TOWARD THE SUN

TOWARD THE SUN

THE COLLECTED SPORTS STORIES OF KENT NELSON

BREAKAWAY BOOKS
NEW YORK CITY
1998

Toward the Sun: The Collected Sports Stories of Kent Nelson

ISBN: 1-891369-05-9
Library of Congress Catalog Card Number: 98-71736

The author wishes to acknowledge the following magazines and to thank their editors, who first published these stories, in slightly altered form: "The Actress" in *Mid-American Review*, "Death Valley" in *Shenandoah*, "A False Encounter" in *The Black Warrior Review*, "Floating" in *The Sewanee Review*, "Instants" in *Transatlantic Review*, "The Invisible" and "Toward the Sun" in *The Missouri Review*, "Projections" in *Confrontation*, "The Squash Player" in *The Virginia Quarterly Review*, "The Tennis Player" in *Michigan Quarterly Review*, and "Winter Ascent" in *Southwest Review*.

Published by Breakaway Books
P.O. Box 1109
Ansonia Station
New York, NY 10023

(800) 548-4348
(212) 595-2216

FIRST EDITION

For my brother, Scott, defense to my offense;

for Danny Hogan, enthusiastic competitor and a believer;

for Q and Berry, squash in the heat;

and for Douglas Cram, whose support has been there,
even in the darkness.

CONTENTS

TOWARD THE SUN

NIEMAN RUNS IN THE MOUNTAINS. HE STARTS FROM OUR SMALL house at 7700 hundred feet, and in a few minutes I see his tattered gray sweat suit drifting among the dark spruce on the Twin Peaks Trail. When I return from the garden with the day's pick of beans, lettuce, and squash—we get no tomatoes at this altitude—he will be coming out of the Oak Creek gorge at 8500 feet. I like to watch him there because the trail skirts through scrub oak and along a cliff, and he is in the open for several minutes until he turns the corner and crosses the meadow into aspens.

I lay the vegetables on the porch step, wipe my hands on my blouse, and pick up the binoculars. In the circle of the glass, Nieman's form is muddled by heat waves from the neighbor's roof, but I do not need perfect focus to be absorbed. Against the red sandstone he holds his arms perpendicular to his body, as if he were a hawk tilting its wings to catch the thermals and updrafts that swirl among the crags. He reaches out with his long legs and steps lightly over the rocky trail, darting as the path twists along the contour of the cliff.

I know his face, the physical strain in the creases of his eyes and in the tight, pursed lips. His distant expression is somnambulant and dreamlike, though Nieman claims he never dreams. I imagine sweat beading on his forehead, oozing into his eyes, and I re-create his face with the serenity

I wish were there. In my leisure, standing by the vegetables, I make him over.

And in Nieman there is much to want to change.

First I would change the legend. The stories about him are both widespread and exaggerated because he neither confirms nor denies the details. To many, Nieman is heroic, superhuman. When he runs he never tires. When he races, which is seldom now, he wins without apparent effort. His stride is longer, his body in better condition than anyone else's. In high school fifteen years ago, he ran a mile in four minutes flat, but when colleges tried to recruit him, he said he couldn't run on level ground. He stayed in the mountains and went to college nearby so he could run as he wanted.

I know Nieman's unusual power. Once I climbed Mount Sneffels with friends from the Blue Lakes side—a seven-mile hike with an elevation gain of almost five thousand feet. We started at eight in the morning, and by three in the afternoon were nearing the summit. Nieman had lunch in town and beat us to the top.

Yet it is not the legend itself that troubles me so much as what it does to Nieman. He does not exactly believe his own press, but the stories have an unsettling effect on him, as if inciting him to further outrages, to harder tasks. To me, his myth is another shadow on a body which already has too many.

When I met Nieman three years ago, I was painting, studying with a man in Santa Fe. I had just begun to discover my own style—a natural affinity for spare colors, for light. I understood space and temporal mood. Perhaps in my personal life I had too much comfort, but I felt strong, and at the time Nieman was on crutches.

"Your fault or his?" I asked, nodding at the cast.

"Man versus machine," he said.

He smiled, but his face was sad. His eyes were uneasy, as though there were in them a tautness or impatience between mind and heart.

"I tried to race a car to an intersection, and I thought the driver was playing the game."

"So it was yours?"

"He never saw me," Nieman said.

At the time, of course, I didn't know Nieman was *that* kind of runner. I assumed he was one of the millions who'd taken to the fad. He was a good-looking man who raced cars to intersections.

I didn't know he was sick.

Sick. Perhaps he's not sick, but a fanatic. A zealot without a cause. I can understand the desire to hone the body to a fine edge, to increase the endurance of the muscles, to strive for greater lung capacity. But those motivations are superfluous to Nieman. His body is already beyond fitness, past the limits of endurance. Perhaps he wants to push away the routine of daily life, to escape. But where? He is in the mountains five or six hours a day. If he could eat and sleep on his feet, he could run forever. No one runs like Nieman simply to take his mind off his problems.

He leaves the cliff edge and climbs to the meadow. His brown hair tufts in the wind, his legs drive effortlessly uphill. His ragged sweatsuit sways and dances against the pale green. He breaks into the clearing and crosses suddenly from the sunlight into the shadow of the dark timber.

Nieman, I know, does not mind the shadow. To him the warmth of the sun and the cold of the shadow are the same.

"Why can't you tell me?" I asked him before he left.

"Tell you what?"

"What you're doing."

He turned away without answer—an admission he is doing something.

He will tell me. He does not keep anything to himself for long, and it is not to lie that he is silent. I cannot accuse him of deception. He has never told me anything false. He is shy and awkward around people, not meant for superficial banter. But he cannot be dishonest. If there were a seed of dishonesty in him, he would, like an oyster, make a pearl of it. That kind of honesty is both hard to come by and hard to endure.

Once I asked what he thought about when he ran. When he was in the mountains alone and felt the mist of the clouds on his face, what did he know? When he skipped over roots and rocks and climbed to the ribbons of snow, he must have thought something.

"No," he said. "I don't think about anything."

"Your mind is blank? Absolutely blank?"

"Not blank, but I don't think of anything."

Then he was silent. He smiled at my wanting to know, and I got angry. If he didn't want to talk that was one thing, but to smile as though I were sweet for asking was another. I suppose it angered me that he knew he did not have to explain himself. I loved him anyway. And the more he was silent, the more I poured myself into his silence.

He's made me quit painting, though not because he's forbidden it. Nieman hasn't said anything. My vision is not so clear in these mountains as it was in Santa Fe. My sense of color is different; light is not the same. The rapport among hand, eye, and the land has withered, and I feel stiff and tentative, even when I sketch. I haven't given it up so much as I'm waiting for a time I don't feel rushed.

I don't delude myself. I know the truth is marred by my caring for Nieman. I have given him too much for safekeeping. What troubles me is not that I have stopped painting for

the moment, but that in my giving I am still not all Nieman
wants or all he needs.

Nieman is a phenomenon as much as a geyser or a meteor.
To treat him as normal would be to admit he is the same as
everyone else. When he runs beside his friends, it's plain
how separate he is. His stride cannot be compared with
theirs. His gait has a different energy. To Nieman's one step,
the others seem to take two.

Nor does Nieman have the distance runner's lanky frame.
His legs are thicker and stronger than the bony-kneed
marathon man's. His upper body is slight, but not sunken as
those who are all lungs. Nieman is bigger. He has sturdy
shoulders and a tapered waist. His arms are long and wiry, and
his thighs raw-muscled. He does not tire when he runs. Ever.

Yet he is generous. When other runners seek his advice,
Nieman gives his time willingly. He would do anything they
asked—lend them money, give his name to causes. Most of
all, though, they want to learn how he does it, and he shares
with them what they believe are secrets. But his running is
not something Nieman has learned and can impart to others.
His body is the marvel, and the running is in him alone.

And yet to treat him as extraordinary doesn't help. All it
does is give him license to disregard the limitations the rest
of us must face. Nieman believes without thinking he can do
whatever he wishes. That is another part of him that ought
to be changed.

He is gone now from the meadow and has moved into the
trees. I pick up the vegetables from the step, survey the
carefully weeded garden and the clean wash on the line—
everything except Nieman's gray running clothes. Lately I
have adopted his strategy of silence, though it isn't my

nature to accept what hurts me. I'm afraid of small things that have meaning. Nieman has let his hair grow. He uses no soap when he showers. He refuses to let me wash his sweat suit or underwear.

And the tenderness in our lovemaking is gone. He holds me fiercely now and presses against me so hard I'm breathless. But in the hurt is a new pleasure: I feel he needs me more.

Do I punish myself? Do I spoil him? Sometimes I want to walk away and give him the freedom to do what he will do without me. But where would I go? I have my garden. The house is now as much mine as his. I'm the one who's expanded the small store from which he used to squeeze out a living. I've brought my brass bed from Santa Fe.

I'm fascinated by the things I know, but he doesn't. I know his body from the outside. Lying on him can be soft, or like lying on marble. He can rock me on his thighs by flexing his legs. My own body gives way. Even now—still—I am surprised how peacefully I sleep against his slow heart.

Nieman says he never dreams, but he wakes in the night running. He babbles in guttural sounds, and he turns toward me with his eyes closed to the moonlight. His body is rigid, and he holds me as if I were a fragile glass figurine. He is dreaming, but when I tell him later what he has done, he says he doesn't remember. He looks away.

I try to talk to him, but he won't listen, or rather, he listens but won't say much in return.

"Are you going to race?" I ask.

"No."

"Travel?"

"You're going with me."

That is all I have.

* * *

He runs with such discipline, though he claims it takes no discipline to do what one truly loves. Sometimes when I wait for him at a certain place on a trail, knowing he has to pass me, he surprises me from behind. How does he do this? When the wind is right, he can do the same to a deer. He can run silently and at full speed.

I wonder whether it's I he runs from. I was twenty-six when I met him; now I'm twenty-nine. Nieman is thirty-three. In three years his body hasn't changed except to become stronger. His leg has healed. He has no trace of a scar or a limp. I think about ski racers, about how speed is as much a function of psychology as of physics. Once speed causes pain, the mind forces the body to be cautious. The racer slows after a break. But with Nieman it is the opposite. His broken leg has encouraged him to take further risks.

And yet we age. Nieman ages. He must know his time is getting shorter. I imagine him at forty, at fifty, still running in the mountains, still tireless. I am glad to watch him now, while my painting is gathering strength in me, but I don't want to watch him forever, seeing my own heart move through time and space. I have limits.

He makes an effort for me. He goes to parties because I enjoy other people. We go to movies. Sometimes on weekends he tosses horseshoes at a barbecue or plays softball, though he is no good at catching or throwing. But these parts of his life mean nothing to him, as if, at the same time he is swinging at a softball, he is seeing another, entirely different configuration of forces from the one others see. Nieman's reality is an undercurrent, another time frame, a dreamwork.

Once when we rode home from a party I asked him about the future.

"I don't see a future," he said.

"But we must have something."

"Who?"

"The two of us."

He raised his eyes from the road and turned to me. He didn't understand.

"I don't mean forever," I said, not wanting to offend him, yet offending myself for worrying. "I mean, we should think about what we may miss and can't get back to."

"Regrets," he said.

"Yes. Sometime I would like to . . . " But the word *child* did not emerge.

The lack of family has something to do with the way Nieman is. He had no antecedents, no parents to look to and see himself. He molds himself to his own image. That's why a child would help him.

I could trick him, of course. Deceiving Nieman would be like deceiving a helpless old man. Nieman would never know. He wouldn't ask whether I meant to get pregnant. If I talked to him openly about our having a child, he'd say no, but if he were confronted with the child's coming, he wouldn't ascribe to me the motive of a lie.

I would be happy if Nieman would change just enough to join my life. He knows I can't wait forever. He can't wait forever. Some say to cage an animal destroys its essence. I have seen a coyote in a zoo pacing back and forth on a sterile concrete floor, gazing through the wire mesh. What kind of animal has it become when it knows it will be fed at intervals, when it is cared for, when it cannot hunt and run free? Is it the same animal I see at the edge of my headlights driving a dark road at night?

If Nieman would change just a little—but then, would he be Nieman?

* * *

II

The air has a nick of autumn on the morning Nieman takes me with him into the mountains. In the high country, the aspens have already edged to yellow. Nieman is unusually quiet. Sometimes when we hike together he speaks of the wildlife or the weather or the history of the mines, but this day he moves quickly along the trail, waiting at intervals for me to catch up. Several times I sense he wants to speak to me. In his face is a strain seldom there. But what he knows he will not tell, and what he will not tell commits us both to silence.

He carries the tent, most of the food, and a thin sleeping bag. I have a lighter pack with a down bag, a pad, aluminum pots, which take up space, and paper on which to sketch if the mood strikes me. The trail skirts the wall of a cliff, drops into a streambed, then rises again into rocky crags. I have been here before: to alpine meadows, steep waves of timber, and up higher to where the trees peter out and cannot grow at all.

Once I stop to rest, and Nieman kisses me and smiles.

"What is it you're going to do?" I ask.

His expression changes. He does not like my directness. Without answering, he starts up again along the trail.

When we reach the end of the second cliff, we move through dark timber for half a mile. Nieman changes again: now he is playful, alert. He acts as though he were leading me through dangerous terrain.

Then finally the high meadows open up before us. The long summer grass has turned dead yellow here, and the hills rise toward benches of yellow-red aspen. Farther away is more dark timber and, above timberline, rocky scree that borders the sky.

Even after we set up our rough camp at the edge of the meadow, Nieman is not at ease. He scans the steep meadows, looking for something, and when I ask what he seeks, he turns away.

That night he makes love to me with a frightening passion, nearly ripping my flesh with his. He does not seem to know me, and I cry out helplessly. Later, when he is quiet, I feel sorry for him, and angry. Why should he torture himself when help is so close by?

In the morning he gets up and wakes himself in the icy stream. He immerses his naked body where I can barely dip my hands. He shouts and splashes and rushes at me laughing, as though to pull me in, but I jump back and run into the meadow.

After breakfast we climb higher. Nieman wears his gray sweatsuit and his running shoes, and he carries nothing. The meadow slopes upward, a steep hill with several glades of aspen. The white bark of the trees is so clean, and a chill comes over me when we enter the halo of yellowing leaves. The trembling heart-shaped leaves make me feel barren.

Nieman stops frequently, still surveying the sides of the valley, still watching the dark timber toward which we climb. Once he pauses abruptly and raises his head.

"What do you see?"

He looks at me strangely, as though caught. "It's what I smell," he says.

I try to catch the scent of whatever it is, but I gather only the aroma of dry grass and a hint of spruce.

We move forward again at a steady pace, but Nieman is now absorbed and deliberate. We pick our way along game trails through another glen of aspen, and beyond into a sunny meadow. But even in the warm sun I feel the cool breeze off the mountain, and the day tightens around my heart.

In the meadow we stop for a snack. Nieman barely eats.

He stares at the rocky scree and the dark timber above us. Seeing what? Knowing what? He looks old.

Then he nods and utters an eerie cry. I follow his gaze.

Elk. I find them easily in the binoculars. There are perhaps thirty of them, mostly light-rumped cows moving slowly uphill, grazing the shreds of grass that are invisible to me from such a distance. Two spike bulls with dark manes escort the cows.

I glance at Nieman, who crouches stock-still.

Then below the elk, from the dark timber, comes a huge antlered bull. He climbs to the others, stops, and turns his head toward us.

Nieman starts running.

It is astonishing how quickly he moves away from me up the sharp angle of the hill. Within a minute he is into the timber, breaking through brush, leaping fallen logs. I call to him, but he does not hear me, or he hears me and does not answer.

I retreat to the edge of the meadow for a better view, and Nieman's gray running suit moves among the spruce. He weaves, ducks branches, then stops suddenly in a shaded clearing. In the binoculars I see him bend down and rub his hands in the dirt. He presses his hands to his clothes, then moves to another place nearby and rolls on the ground. He lifts handfuls of dirt and spruce needles and rubs them over his face.

It dawns on me what he is doing. Perhaps I have known before, but I realize it at that moment in my heart: the distraction, the running, the silences. He breaks from the clearing and climbs into the trees. I nearly call to him again, but it would be of no use even were I to scream.

It takes me half an hour to reach the opening in the trees where Nieman's tracks are. I find the markings on the ground where he gathered the dirt in his hands. I touch the earth to confirm what I know and lift my hands to my nostrils. The smell is everywhere, sickening, so strong it's horror. The odor is of elk urine and the musk of elk beds recently deserted.

From the cover of the trees I can see nothing so I move higher, aching, knowing how Nieman smells. The game trails are overgrown, and I fight my way through the underbrush. The branches scrape me, catch my anger, but I gain higher ground. Gray granite peaks surround me, and beneath and across stretch the deep valleys where snow lies in perpetual shadow.

I scan the slopes for several minutes before I see the elk again. They have already moved a mile or more into another drainage. The hills dividing each ravine are lines of yellow and gray, one beyond another, sliding downward toward the stream. The elk skirt these hills, running now, sensing the danger behind them.

Then Nieman appears just below the line of the ridge. In the binoculars I see the thin game trail he follows, and as seconds elapse, he becomes clearer. His stride is forceful, strong yet graceful. The tension in his face is gone.

The elk cannot see him around the curve of the hill, and he cannot see them. But each knows the other is there. Nieman runs in their tracks. His legs carry him easily, for Nieman never tires. The expression on his face is dreamlike, though Nieman claims he never dreams.

Watching him, I feel a lightness seep into me—weakness and strength. I gaze around: the high country is as foreign as a bleak moon.

The elk run along the base of a huge crag, descend into another valley, then climb higher toward the saddle between two peaks. For a time Nieman closes the gap, but the elk move faster. After a few minutes, they tire, and Nieman gains.

He holds his head straight. His legs reach out, and his arms churn smoothly. I imagine his body beneath the sweat-suit, the sweat mingling with the urine and musk of elk. I wonder whether our child would have Nieman's body, Nieman's elk body, Nieman's resolve.

The elk ascend the last pitch to the saddle, and in the angle of the sun become part light and part silhouette as they disappear over the pass. I shiver and turn away before Nieman reaches the top.

THE SQUASH PLAYER

ART MCNEAL WOKE AT FOUR O'CLOCK TUESDAY MORNING with a sharp pain in his lower back. He tossed and winced for half an hour before his wife, Muriel, turned over and said, "For God's sake, Art, go to sleep."

He got up and went to the bathroom, where he checked himself in the full-length mirror. Not a mark: his ribbed back showed no cut or bruise. He turned around and stared for a moment at his sleep-swollen face and the tiny lines at the corners of his eyes. Back trouble was no joke. He knew men far younger than he who couldn't play tennis or golf or even jog. He tried bending back and forth, but the pain restricted him to swaying. He got into the shower and turned the dial spigot toward hot.

Muriel came into the bathroom with her robe on and got a glass of water. Art leaned from behind the shower curtain.

"What's with you?" she asked.

"Back."

"From the squash?"

He shook his head. "I must have slept on it wrong." He stepped boldly from the shower and grabbed a towel from the rack. "It hurts, though."

Muriel rummaged through the untidy medicine cabinet filled with vials, small containers, bottles. "Maybe there's some liniment here," she said.

"It needs heat," Art said.

Muriel held up a bottle of pills. "I have a prescription drug for pain," she said. "Dr. Grogan gave it to me last summer when I had that inflammation."

Art refused her with a stare. Her hair was lighter than whenever he'd last noticed it, more frosted blond than gray. (He'd asked many times whether it was the sun or frosted at Yvonne's.) She looked healthy enough otherwise—thin body, good legs, which somehow she maintained without exercise.

"Anything to make you sleep," she said.

"I'll go sleep in Janie's room."

She touched his arm and smiled. "Have you thought you may finally be getting old?"

The afternoon before, he had played seven games of tough squash with Terdell Hardy, who'd been on the Williams team four years ago. Although Art was a good dozen years older, he'd won four games, including the last two. No one was in better shape than he was. Art made the squash team at Yale only in his senior year, and then only at number nine, but he was a tenacious competitor. What he lacked in natural ability he made up in sheer speed and hustle. He could run forever from corner to corner, from front wall to back. He threw himself at corner kills to keep the ball alive even though he knew the next shot would end the point. At Yale he led the team in broken racquets, trying to return perfect side-wall huggers. His theory was if he could keep the ball in play long enough, his enemy would make a mistake. Some shot was better than no shot.

Janie's bed was no help. Her room was cold and unfamiliar and too quiet. Besides, Art worried about her not being there. Whenever he found a comfortable position without pain, he had visions of his daughter as the victim of a heinous crime. He imagined her being accosted as she walked to class in her green school uniform, or molested as she hitchhiked into Boston. He saw her body lying in a leafy woodland with her throat slit. Then he rolled over and moaned from the pain in his back.

He blamed Muriel for the decision to send her away. Muriel's theory was that private school would awaken the dormant intellectual seed. In another environment, Janie could flourish. Art swore fourteen was too young to be away from home. If Janie spent less time listening to Twisted Sister and The Rat Boys, her grades would improve. It made him uneasy that from such a distance—Connecticut to Massachusetts—he could not vouch for her safety.

He supposed he'd protected her too much, had allowed her too much. Not that she had been trouble in the normal sense: she'd never been wild or openly hostile, had never done drugs. She malingered. She waited till the last minute to do her homework; she was late getting home from friends' houses; when she played tennis, she ran around her backhand and didn't chase down balls she could easily have got to. She couldn't improve, he said, if she took the path of least resistance.

She hitchhiked sometimes, despite his forbidding it, and when he warned her not to, she said, "Okay, Daddy." He showed her clippings from newspapers about rapes and murders. "Think about the consequences," he told her.

"I will," she said.

Then she did it again.

What worried him most was that she was pretty. Muriel had been pretty, too. Both boys and girls sought Janie's company. Good looks led to alternatives, alternatives to equivocation, and equivocation ultimately to sadness and destruction.

Art sat up in bed. The night had sifted away, and the room slowly took shape and color. Janie's bookshelf—mostly empty—divided the far wall into squares. Janie had left two posters on the wall adjacent: had she thought too little of them to take them with her to school, or too much? One was a blowup of Eric Clapton with a yellow flash highlighting his guitar and his electric hair. The other was a sunrise photograph over dunes and water, captioned in Gothic scrawl with the platitude TODAY IS THE FIRST DAY OF THE REST OF YOUR LIFE.

With effort he got up and opened the lacy curtains. The spiny tips of the trees behind the house were outlined in silver against the darker hill beyond. During the night the frost had turned the grass white, and the small black stream that flowed along the border of their property was frozen at the edges where the current ran more slowly. He was surprised that through the tangled patch of brush and trees he could see two other houses.

Janie's huge circular mirror reflected gray from the window's dawn, and Art watched himself pace in the gathering light. He was short—five-eight (which he neither liked nor accepted)—and his body was finely muscled. He needed no discipline to stay fit: squash was as much exercise as anyone needed. He rotated his shoulders and held out his arms, palms up. From years of racquet sports, his right forearm was thicker than his left. He pressed a hand against his back to push away the pain.

Years ago, he'd persuaded Muriel a second child would benefit all of them, Janie particularly. Turning all the parental energy on one child was like focusing a magnifying glass on dry tinder. Besides, he wanted to change the odds. With one child, it was all or nothing.

Muriel had acquiesced. At least he thought she had. Janie was two, and his career in investment banking had been on the upswing. But Muriel hadn't conceived. He'd begged her to see a doctor.

"Why do you think it's me?" she asked.

Nothing had happened, and gradually, as Janie got older, this psychological argument paled. But even as lately as last spring, he'd brought up the subject again. He remembered she was setting out wine glasses on the table for a dinner party.

"We tried, Art," Muriel said. "I don't think it's so critical for Janie now."

"It might help us."

"I'm too old," Muriel said. "Statistically, women nearing forty have a smaller chance of giving birth to healthy children."

"You're thirty-six," he said. "You have lots of years."

She'd finished setting the wine glasses out and got a trayful of water tumblers. "Art, my life is tolerable now. For the moment I don't have any desire to change it so you can feel proud of your virility." She handed him the tray of glasses. "Here, put these on the table."

"My virility has nothing to do with it. And what do you mean, 'for the moment'?"

"Just what I said."

At six-thirty Muriel called up the stairs that he would be late for his morning train into the city.

"I'm not going," he called back.

Muriel's footsteps came up the stairs and she entered Janie's room. He was still naked, standing by the window. Muriel was dressed in a pair of green slacks and a gray ski sweater, and she was already made up. "Are you really hurt?" she asked.

"I can't work," he said. "I'll have to call Muncie." He fell onto the bed, and a long sliver of pain shot along his spine.

"Maybe you can get me some Atomic Balm."

She gazed at him calmly, as though she were impatient with his imagining. "Anything else, your lordship?"

"I guess not."

"If it's that bad," she said, "you should call Dr. Grogan."

"Look . . ." He felt slighted, and his temper flared.

"I'll be back as soon as I can."

He dozed, then woke when his dream got scary. He had taken Janie to the park. She was only eight or so, her hair in tight blond curls. She wore a short-sleeved yellow dress. He watched her run across the path, leaves fluttering, dappled in the sunlight. Shadows lay behind her. Colors flashed to his eye—the yellow dress, the green leaves—then suddenly the red coat of a man chasing her with a knife. Art sprinted toward Janie. He was at an angle to her, but he was too late: the man with the knife moved away.

The shock of his dream took several minutes to ease, slipping away as his heart resumed its steady beating. He couldn't recall anytime in the match with Terdell Hardy when he had pulled a back muscle. He could have understood a trauma, but he hated the void of not knowing. At an office picnic years before he'd played soccer, and for three days afterward, he could barely move. But that was explainable: soccer utilized different muscles. He was in shape to play squash.

He closed his eyes again, only to be shaken by the chiming bell of Janie's telephone. He sat up and answered. "Hello?"

The line was quiet for several seconds, and then the caller hung up. Art frowned and laid the Princess in its cradle.

The small pennant he'd given Janie for her birthday (to inspire her) was still tacked to the wall above her dresser, together with other mementos she had outgrown. Fifteen now. She would, of course, be back at Christmas: school was not *that* far away. But it made him sad not to see her every day. The child had so much potential. She had tested in the ninety-eighth percentile in the public school, and she could easily have been near the top of her class wherever she went. Potential: a tough word to define. Could do, might have done. When did it change?

Muriel, for example, had potential. She had grown up in a close family of painters and pianists and had inherited both temperament and talent. When she sat at the piano her hands glided over the keyboard pulling flight, breezes, despair from the music. Art wished she would play again. She had such a gift. What might she have done if, long before, she had given herself to the world of concert music instead of marrying him?

She had stopped playing when Janie was born. The house had suddenly emptied of music, and it took him by surprise. He'd thought when Janie's needs subsided, Muriel would resume playing, but she hadn't.

"I'd be glad to listen," he'd said more than once.

"I haven't got time to practice."

"Well, make time. If you . . ."

"I don't feel like it," she said.

End of subject.

Janie had never learned the piano because Muriel had not pressed her, which was a puzzlement to Art. Muriel had said not to push. But potential needed pushing. Janie was smart. If she had talent, why shouldn't she develop it? The trouble was that potential washed away as quickly as a footprint in the sand.

In Art's own case, potential had not mattered so much as perseverance. He was a plodder and knew it, bright enough to do well if he worked hard. He might have preferred a career in publishing to the one he had chosen in investment banking, but he never permitted himself regret. What was the point? Once in a while he still thought of his grandfather's printing shop—the whine and roll of the presses, the smudged aprons of the men who wore green, plastic-brimmed caps, the acrid and tantalizing smell of ink. But those were the old days. His grandfather had sold the business when Art's father had been injured in an automobile crash. The important thing, his grandfather said, was to pay the bills.

The electric clock beside Janie's bed changed: eight-zero-nine. Eight-ten. Art called his secretary at the office and told her he was sick.

He hated lying in bed. No matter what the pain was like he wanted to be up and doing something, anything—digging in the garden, raking leaves, running. Except for the maddeningly thin line between comfort and agony, he felt fine.

Through the skeleton of the house he heard the remote-control garage door open and close. Then the telephone chimed again. He waited for Muriel to answer, and when she didn't, he lifted the receiver quietly and said nothing.

"Muriel?"

The man's voice was familiar, but Art couldn't place it. "Who's this?"

The caller hung up abruptly.

It was an eternity before Muriel reached the oak floor in the hall. Her footsteps echoed. She passed through to the kitchen. After a few minutes he heard the washing machine thumping. It was another ten minutes before she climbed the stairs and came into Janie's room with her tote bag over her arm. She hadn't taken off her coat yet.

"Where were you?" Art asked sullenly.

"I took some books back to the library and got you one on squash."

"Squash? I know how to play squash."

"I saw Misty at the jeweler's and talked to her for a while. I left Janie's pendant to be fixed. Then I went by the pharmacy, and now I've started a load of wash. That's where I've been."

"You put in laundry at this hour?"

"Today's laundry day," Muriel said. She opened her tote bag and took out the Atomic Balm. "Do you want me to put this on your back?"

He scrutinized her face for some sign of sympathy, but the cool lines around her mouth and radiating from her eyes did not alter their configuration. He threw back the covers gingerly and turned over onto his stomach.

"And all this time I thought you were so rugged," she said.

The strategy in squash was to control the tee. If you kept your opponent behind you and in the corners, he couldn't attack. It was like physical chess: any small advantage was pressed relentlessly until it became a decisive lead. Position was critical. Since both players hit to the front wall, the center was avidly contested. The jostling of bodies, nudging, collisions were part of the game. Art liked the closeness and the feeling of a sweat-soaked shirt on his back, the squeak of shoes, the wearing down of the opposition.

Success was quickness and guile. Art had a good drop shot, a fair boast, but it was conditioning that enabled him to retrieve everything his opponent could hit. And he had great deception. Nothing gave him more satisfaction than wrong-footing his opponent, seeing him streak forward when Art hit a lob, or leaning for the rail when Art hit a reverse corner.

* * *

Muriel set breakfast on the bed on a tray: poached eggs on toast, ham, cereal, orange juice. "Are you better?" she asked.

Art didn't answer.

"Maybe you should come back downstairs to our room," she said. "Janie's doesn't suit you."

"How could you get me a book on squash?" he asked.

"I thought you'd like it."

Art glanced at her to judge her motive. Was the book a not-very-subtle dig, or was she perfectly innocent? If she was innocent, how could she be? Hadn't he told her about his matches? But she had moved into that intractable age when she was still pretty, but noticeably older, and her face gave away nothing. "I like it here," he said.

"Did the heat help?" She crossed to the window and pulled the curtains slightly against the changing angle of the sun. The washing machine hammered on the spin cycle, and his pain conformed to the throbbing in the walls.

"Have you ever thought about moving?" Art asked.

"What do you mean?"

"Buying another house. Pulling up stakes. Frank Lloyd Wright said when you can see your neighbors' houses you should go farther into the country."

"Where would we go?" Muriel asked. "Where is farther into the country than here?"

"I don't know. Seattle. They play good squash in Seattle."

"You can't play squash forever," Muriel said, "and Frank Lloyd Wright is dead. Anyway, Seattle is hardly the country."

"Then you like it here?"

"Yes, of course. Why?"

Art shrugged and took a bite of poached egg and toast.

* * *

"What do you think it is?" Art asked. He was lying on the examining table in Dr. Grogan's office.

Dr. Grogan shook his head and moved around the foot of the table to Art's shoulder. He was slightly older than Art, paunchy, soft skinned. He looked over his half-glasses. "Can you sit up?"

Art sat up, and Dr. Grogan shone a light into Art's eyes.

"It's not my eyes," Art said.

"Look past me." Dr. Grogan leaned closer. "I didn't say it was your eyes."

Dr. Grogan checked Art's ears and throat and listened to his heart for what seemed to Art like ten minutes.

"Now this pain you say is in your lower back?"

"Right here." Art stretched his hand around his waist and felt a knife slice through him.

"You can use words," Dr. Grogan said. "You first noticed it this morning?"

"I played squash yesterday afternoon," Art said. "I beat Terdell Hardy four out of seven. The pain came early this morning."

Dr. Grogan pressed the lumbar region with his fingertips, and Art held himself steady. "Lie back down, please."

Art lay back on the cold table. The doctor raised each of Art's legs and pressed it toward his stomach.

"All I want is a pill," Art said. "Just to get back to normal."

Dr. Grogan tested his reflexes with his hammer, stuck pins into his feet, made notes on his clipboard chart. "You can get dressed now," he said.

Dr. Grogan took out a prescription pad and sat down at a small table. Art climbed down and slipped on his slacks.

"It seems to be a virus," Dr. Grogan said, glancing up from his pad.

"What kind of virus?"

"A virus is a mystery almost by definition. There's nothing we can do for it, but these capsules should ease the pain and let you sleep."

"I don't want to sleep," Art said. "I want a cure."

"You seem to have a form of lumbar neuralgia which usually strikes older people. I'd caution you about these pills . . ."

"Are you suggesting I'm old?" Art slid on his shirt with some discomfort.

Dr. Grogan smiled briefly. "There's no cure in the sense of a cure for disease. Your body has to fight the virus."

"How 'ong?"

"It may take weeks, maybe months."

"But it goes away?"

"In the usual case it goes away."

Art buttoned his shirt and, ignoring the proffered prescription, walked out of the examining room.

When he got home, Muriel was out. He mixed himself a rum and tonic and sat with the morning paper in the bay window overlooking the backyard. He did not care that inflation might be worsening or that another taxi strike threatened the city. It hurt like hell to hold the newspaper with his arms outstretched so he could read it.

Finally he folded the paper and stared into the hazy, gray, leafless trees on the horizon.

The telephone rang, but he didn't answer it. Five minutes later, it rang again. He got it in the kitchen on the sixth ring. "Hello," he said.

"Hello?" The voice was a woman's.

"Yes?"

"I have a collect call from Jane McNeal. Will you pay for the call?"

He took a breath, "Of course. Janie?"

"Hello?" Janie's voice came on, mixed with the noise of traffic.

"Hello, Janie."

"Dad, what are you doing home? Is Mom there?"

"Which question should I answer first?"

"Is she there?" Janie asked. There was a rise in her voice.

"No, I don't know where she is."

Janie paused on the other end of the line. "Jeez . . ."

"Can I help?" Art asked. "Where are you?"

"School."

Art knew she was lying from her tone of voice, not to mention the traffic in the background. "Where?" he asked.

"Do you know whether Mom's written me?" Janie asked.

"No. Is there some kind of trouble?" A car honked in the background. "Are you all right?"

"I'm *fine*."

"You don't sound fine."

"No, really, I'm okay. My schoolwork's better. It's not such a bad place, I guess. How are you and Mom getting along?"

"We get along very well. Why do you ask that?"

"Do you have the day off?"

"Not exactly. I have a backache."

"Listen," Janie said. "I have to go. Could you have Mom call me?"

"Sure I can, honey, but . . ."

"Thanks," Janie said. "Bye."

Art stood with the telephone pressed tightly against his neck where the blood pounded in a vein.

He hung up and went to Muriel's desk in the den and looked through her papers for a letter to Janie. He found a couple of notes from her sister, one from a college friend, some bills and catalogs—nothing that, if he'd paid attention, he might not have known about. He opened a small drawer in the center and, under some bank statements, found a scribble of Janie's. Her handwriting never had been very good. It was postmarked five days before—obviously it had been hidden. Janie had asked her mother to send five hundred dollars.

By four that afternoon Art was drunk. With each rum and tonic, he increased the proportion of rum. On his way back from making his fifth, he knocked over a small table and kicked it against the wall, shattering three of its legs. The pain in his back and the rum made him rage.

He'd been upstairs and had torn apart Janie's room looking for some clue. He searched the pockets of her summer clothes, had gone through every drawer in her dresser, every book and record on her shelf—hoping to find what? Drugs? A diary?

Finding nothing made him furious.

Downstairs he had looked more carefully through Muriel's desk. He hadn't tried to hide his act, but instead had tossed letters, pencils, drawerfuls of checks and receipted bills across the den. Finally he had sought out the morning newspaper and ripped it apart, too, spreading crumpled sheets across the porch and the living room.

He sat amid the debris, drinking and waiting for Muriel to get home. The house was cold, but he didn't get up to turn up the heat. A shadow descended from the western hill, darkening the trees and the yard. He was surprised how early dusk fell in the country, and how quickly, once it had begun, the colors faded.

Then Muriel was in the kitchen rustling grocery bags, opening cupboard doors. "Art?"

He hadn't heard the garage door or her footsteps on the

basement stairs.

"Art?" She came into the living room and stopped.

He gazed at her across the sea of crumpled newspapers and lifted his glass. "Terminal illness," he said. "Death awaits."

"My God, what is going on here?" Muriel didn't move. "What did the doctor say, really?"

"Goes away," Art said. "Usual case." He swept his hand through the air along a slope from top to bottom. "Fades away." He paused to see whether she had changed in any way since that morning. Her lipstick looked fresh; her short hair was neat. She still had on her green slacks and gray sweater.

She clicked across the wooden floor to the den. "My desk," she said. "What were you doing in there?"

He took a long drink. "Research," he said. "Janie called."

His mind whirled with the rum. He alternated between questions and accusations, between shouting and whispering. Muriel's contention was she should not betray Janie, who had discussed matters in confidence.

"What the hell does that mean?" Art asked.

"Privacy. You know damned well what that means. You violated it." She crossed the room to the piano bench and sat down facing him.

"I have a right to know."

"We have a right to secrets."

Art stood and stared out the bay window into the darkened woodland. The pain in his back expanded outward like a speck of light growing steadily brighter and brighter. His shoulders tightened; his legs were numb. He wanted to see Janie, to tell her what he had done and why, to explain he loved her, to ask . . . but he could not move because of the pain.

He stepped back from the window and gazed at his reflection. The shadowed black sockets of his eyes were hollow, and he turned slowly toward Muriel. "And you?" he asked. "How long has this been going on?"

He spent the night in Janie's room amid the piles of clothes, records, books, torn posters. He lay on the bed still dressed, with his eyes open. Dizziness, pain, snatches of conversation filled the waking hours. Sometimes he hung on the edge of sleep, but always he moved so he was conscious of the pain. Once, after hours of grim detail, he slid into the reverie of a game of squash. He entered the white court with his towel around his neck, a roll of tape, his racquet and ball. A wave of nausea at the whiteness swept through him. The walls, the division of wall from ceiling and floor, were vague, blurred. The red lines that defined the game were meaningless, mere decorations on the optical illusion in which he found himself. He walked tentatively. If he moved too quickly he was certain to overstep the limits of the room: he would strike the solid white plane of space. Even the black softball vanished when he swung at it. He concentrated on the bounce, confident his senses would clear. His body took over, gaining a rhythm, as if he were playing a long point, a rally that never ended. He ran from corner to corner. His opponent controlled the T effortlessly, volleying side-wall shots. Art chased down lobs, drops shots, lunged for blistering rails. White emanated from every angle.

Art sat up suddenly, chilled. He got up and went to the window. The night was very cold, and he searched among the moonlit trees for an owl or a leaf's falling. Nothing moved. The strange web of branches and shadows pressed into his mind. Frost was forming again on the grass. Little by little, invisibly, the stream was freezing.

* * *

He came downstairs at six-thirty. The empty rum bottle and the crumpled newspapers had been removed, and the room was clean. Muriel's desk was neat again. The shattered table lay on the landing to the basement steps.

He changed his clothes in their bedroom, where Muriel lay asleep. He put on a suit and tied his tie in front of the mirror. Muriel woke.

"You're going to work?" she asked.

"Yes."

"The back?"

"Better." He lifted the knot of his tie to the V of his collar. "I'm sorry about last night."

He leaned down and kissed her. Then he picked up his shoes and went downstairs to make breakfast.

On his way to the garage he carried the broken table to Muriel's car. He pressed the garage button, and the slatted door rolled up like an eyelid. He walked down the driveway for the newspaper.

His breath, wisps of fog, dissipated in the cold air. The grass was white. The tree branches were rimed with frost. He shivered, for he had worn no coat.

His train was late, but he waited patiently on the platform. When it arrived, he boarded and found a seat as usual. It was early still. He stared out the window, waiting for the train to leave, at the houses and the countryside, then leaned forward over the newspaper in his lap and held his body tightly against the pain.

WINTER ASCENT

AT TEN O'CLOCK AT NIGHT IT WAS SNOWING HARD AT NINE thousand feet. The wind blew across the ridge from the northwest, driving the snow into the corners of the windows and against the thin walls of the A-frame. Bill Tyms was asleep in the loft under the roof, and between the rushes of wind, Pratt heard snoring.

"What's it doing outside now?" Werner asked, smiling at his own joke. He was sitting on a chair near the wall playing solitaire. He was a darkly tanned German from Feldafing, thirty years old, with experience in the Alps. In winter he taught skiing in Telluride, but his love was climbing mountains. "Want to play gin? It'll take your mind off the weather."

"I don't want my mind off the weather."

Pratt shook his head and stared out the window. Twenty feet from the cabin the stand of spruce was hidden by snow.

He was glad Marcy hadn't come with them. She had wanted to send them off from the base camp, but they had been there two days already waiting for the weather to break.

What she really wanted was to make the ascent herself, but he hadn't wanted her to. "It has nothing to do with you," he'd said when they talked about it in town, "and everything to do with me."

"You have to get over that."

"Someday maybe I will."

He turned from his own shadowed reflection in the glass and crossed the wooden floor to his pack. He had checked his equipment in town and again when they arrived at the A-frame, but he wanted to be sure everything was there. Stoppers, pitons for rock and screws for ice, crampons, rope, hard hat, waterproof matches, Primus stove, down jacket, miniflares.

"You think the pack rats have taken something?" Werner asked.

"I'm just checking."

"We're all on edge," Werner said.

"Not Tyms."

"Tyms is on edge in his own way."

The tin roof, warmed from the inside, shed its burden of snow. The slide woke Tyms.

"Fucking snow," Tyms said. "I was dreaming I was on a beach in Jamaica."

"You dream this without rum?" Werner asked.

Tyms stretched his lanky body and dangled his legs over the edge of the loft.

"With three women," Tyms said. "One of them was Marcy."

"That proves it was a dream," Pratt said.

A gust of wind burst against the wall, and the kerosene lantern swung back and forth, throwing garish shadows across the room. Tyms rubbed his eyes and put on his rimless glasses. "What time is it?"

"Past ten."

"Outside temp?"

Pratt leaned toward the window. "Sixteen degrees."

Tyms jumped down from the loft. He was the best of them on ice, a master skater in total control. But on the wooden floor in his long underwear, he looked ghostlike. "How's Pratt holding up?" he asked Werner.

"Great," Pratt said.

"He misses Marcy," Werner said.

"Fuck Marcy," Pratt said.

"My sentiments exactly," Tyms said, leering, showing the gap of his missing lower tooth. "Let me know when you're done with her."

The wind stopped, and the silence tightened the small space. Tyms went to the stove and put in two pieces of spruce. "The clouds will lift in the morning," he said, "and when it's clear, it's going to be cold as a nun's mammary up there."

From town the mountain looked more like a steeply rising jet than a mountain. It soared up nearly eight thousand feet from the valley, and although it was surrounded by other peaks, it was the highest and seemed unreachable. That was why Pratt was fascinated. The land sloped upward from miles away, then jutted into a high plateau. Above the plateau, the dry foothills broke into dozens of ravines and canyons. The view of the mountain—that was what made Pratt stand so many hours at his bedroom window.

In high school he'd run from the trailhead to the ridge without stopping, his thin legs dancing up the zigzags and his breath coming in short gulps. His fingers were so strong he scaled thirty-foot cinder-block walls, holding himself like a spider in the niches of cement. He spent nearly all his free time with Tyms in the mountains.

And at night, when he should have been sleeping, he pressed his face to the cold cracked glass of the bedroom window. The sun never reached the crevasses on the north face, so in all seasons the mountain was etched in white. A cornice lay just below the summit, a thin spine that outlined the northwest buttress. In winter the face was dark, and wind whipped the granite too steep to hold snow. Pratt liked the clean line of snow broken by the crack in his window-pane: two horizons, one higher and one lower, each with the dead night beyond.

"I'm going out," Pratt said. He opened the door and pushed his way into the wind. He fastened the leather latch and moved off several paces to urinate. The frail light from the cabin faded into the gauze of the snow, and heavy flakes nicked his face.

When he finished peeing, he walked up the nose of the ridge into the immense web of darkness and snow. He liked the feeling of the clouds around him, the flakes invisible, the sensation that he was suspended with no mountain above him, no town below, no ridge on which he stood. He knew the mountain better than anyone else alive. When he met Marcy, he was twenty-seven and had climbed to the summit eight times.

He and Tyms had climbed the south face on a clear, cold day on the first of January. The sun had burned them on the snowfield in the basin.

Now: waiting. He hated waiting. That was the trouble with him. The weather, the days going by. The snow.

Or Marcy.

Three nights before—it seemed longer than that—she'd been lying on the bed facing him, the smooth curve of her hip raised beneath the white sheet. He made out the pale shape of her face, but he could not see her eyes. "Why are you so afraid?" she asked.

"Am I afraid?"

"It's not what you say. It's the way you hesitate when you do things, the way you look."

"Then don't watch me."

"But that won't change anything." She'd turned onto her

back and stared at the ceiling. "Tyms said . . ." She paused. "It worries me you'll never get beyond where you are now."

"Tyms said what?"

"He's your friend," she said. "He worries about you, too."

She'd not said anything more and drifted into sleep, leaving him wondering and angry. How was it she slept so easily?

The snow let up, and above him stars drifted in the blackness. Clearing, but snow still blew over the ridge. Spindrift. A cold mist wet his skin.

He turned and waded through the snow, back toward the clearer light of the A-frame.

Pratt kicked snow from his boots at the door and went inside.

"How is it out there?" Werner asked.

"Lovely."

The warmth of the room swarmed into Pratt's face. He went to the stove and turned his hand over the barrel.

"You okay, really?" Tyms asked.

"It's breaking," Pratt said. "We can start in the morning."

Marcy was tall, with long, straight brown hair and a wide-lipped mouth that turned ambiguously whenever she asked a question. He liked her right away: that much was simple. When she walked into his mountaineering store for information about the mountain, he offered to take her up.

She smiled and answered, "No, thank you. I want to go alone."

Still, he spent time with her going over the routes—maps and photographs. He cautioned her about the outcroppings that looked promising but led nowhere, about the places where objective dangers—falling rocks, ice—were worst. She listened carefully, absorbed everything he said, as if his words were all she wanted. And all the time he spoke about the mountain he was feeling something else.

When she was ready, he hiked with her to the base and watched her start. She was in control of herself. On the first pitch of a strange place she knew the rock. She kept herself in perfect position, and her timing was immaculate. She never lacked strength to do what she wanted.

In their three years together, she'd left him many times to climb other mountains; twice she left him for good. The trouble between them was never drawn in clear terms, never discussed so openly as that. Marcy planned her own life; sometimes she invited him to join her, sometimes not. For months they lived well and calmly, and then suddenly one morning she woke up and told him she was leaving for Wyoming. Or Alaska. Or South America.

"You could warn me," he said after the second time, when she'd said she was going to the Yukon to climb Mount Logan.

She shook her head. "No, I can't."

"When are you coming back?"

"I'll have to see."

He tried to take humor in her tone, but at the moment she was serious. Her hair was pulled back, and her mouth was set in a hard line. Her eyes looked too tired for humor.

"What is it you don't want to come back to?" he asked.

"I didn't say that."

"We're so easy."

She nodded. "Yes, that's part of it. We get along too well."

That time she was gone two months, but she came back.

Another time, when she went to South America to do Chimborazo, she said she wasn't coming back. But she did. One day she was home again without a word. She collected her mail, said hello to friends, kissed him hello as if she hadn't been away. God, he loved her. When he was with her he forgot she'd do the same thing again.

* * *

Pratt led through the scraggly trees near timberline, though he could not see the trees until he was a few feet from them. The beam of his lantern caromed from the rough shapes of rock and gnarled branches. The wind had blown the ridge clean of snow, and for the first mile and a half they hiked easily. Tyms kept the pace with his fluid stride; Werner moved doggedly in the rear.

Orion slid wide to the edge of the morning sky, the belt tilted at an angle to the horizon. A few clouds moved across the stars, as if the wind were sweeping the sky clean. Tyms had been right: it was cold. Pratt's feet were already hurting, and as he walked he curled his fingers into fists inside his gloves.

They rested at the boulder field at the base of the mountain. A pale blue light spread through the air.

"We're behind schedule," Tyms said. "It'll be light before we get up the first pitch."

"Who was sleeping late?" Werner asked.

"I'm sorry," Pratt said. "You could have woke me."

"The weather's good," Tyms said. "We're all right."

Pratt looked up past the boulder field. It would be slow going on the snow-slick rock and hard to make out where to step. He felt tired, too, as if the sleep hadn't done any good. Tyms led across the snow with Werner in his tracks. The colors of the parkas—Werner's orange and Tyms's red—separated from the gray dawn.

He never understood how his own crisis began. There was no particular moment, no incident. Climbing one day in the Uncompahgre Gorge, he felt shaky; he sweated profusely on free climbs he did frequently; his arms felt heavy; his fingers ached.

"Old Pratt," Tyms said. "That's what happens when you

get married."

"It's not that."

"What's the doctor say?"

"Everything checks out."

"A batting slump," Tyms said. "You have to keep taking your swings."

Pratt trained harder. He ran Twin Peaks, the Chief Ouray Mine, to Horsethief meadow before he opened the store in the morning. He kept weights in the back room so when business was slow he could exercise. In the afternoons he made technical climbs in Box Canyon and the gorge.

"Maybe you should rest," Marcy said.

Pratt climbed the first pitch after the boulder field and belayed for Werner and Tyms. The early-morning sky deepened, cold as blue ice. Only Venus was left in the east; Orion was gone. Clouds strung out along the backbone of peaks to the west.

Pratt angled to his left, skirted an outcropping of cold stone, wedged a stopper into a crack. His planned route followed a broken line to a couloir, then over ice and snow to the east where they'd reach the ridge into the center of the north face. The route was burned into his mind, fixed in drawings he had gone over with Tyms and Werner. In summer, he'd done the same route in shirtsleeves.

Tyms ran the couloir in crampons, setting ice screws for the others, and leapfrogging. Pratt hesitated before he started out, warmed his hands.

"You can do it," Tyms called across. "We've got the net below you."

Pratt smiled grimly and edged out. After a few steps he got a rhythm and made it easily.

Werner, though, had trouble. He began happily with a

shout, but the noise brought down a wash of snow that swept him off his feet. Tyms laughed when Werner bounced on the belay, but Werner moved his arm gingerly in a circle before he climbed back up to them.

"Shoulder caught a spur," he said.

"If Werner's hurt, we'll all drop back," Pratt said. "No risks."

"We'll rest," Tyms said. "He's all right."

They sat in the lee of the ridge and watched the sun's halo beyond the low hills to the east. Pratt ate a granola bar and passed around cups of hot chocolate he'd heated on the Primus.

"How's it feel?" Pratt asked Werner.

"Okay. It'll work itself out."

Pratt led into the center of the face. It was bare rock, almost vertical, and too steep for snow, and they made only fifty feet in twenty minutes because Werner was hurting. He winced when he reached, and he couldn't lift his weight without effort.

"It's no use," he said. "I'm going down."

Pratt and Tyms agreed; they didn't argue with Werner. But neither did they want to turn back. They had trained and planned and believed and waited.

"You go on," Werner said. "I'll be okay."

But they couldn't leave Werner there.

"We'll take you across the couloir," Tyms said. "You can rappel from there to the boulder field."

"Not a problem," Werner said. "I'll have dinner ready when you get back."

They belayed for Werner across the couloir and again on his rappel. It was an hour lost before they retraced their steps.

A long fault slashed a scar upward—a two-hundred-foot

chimney on a steep angle to their right. The sun glanced from planes of rock, from patches of snow. Pratt moved with his old ease, the muscles lifting, grasping, pulling. The sprints, the work on icefalls, the isometrics: he was alive in the rock. But the mind was difficult to train.

Fatigue.

Cold.

Height.

Fear.

Death.

Marcy said when she climbed she never thought of falling. She was in an automobile accident once, a head-on at sixty, and as the cars collided, she had not thought about the end of her life. The same with falling: in the Dolomites she was struck by a rock and fell five hundred feet with her head tucked and her ice ax across her chest. Her backpack hit rocks twice, and then she hit a hillside and rolled. She said she thought only about being alive.

Pratt had never thought about death, either, when he started climbing. Even now he didn't worry about it consciously. But he felt the possibility. It could happen. Werner could have snapped the belay rope. It was not a dream. Death was in every minute, every second around him, sifting into his brain the way oxygen was absorbed through the lungs into the blood.

"I've never seen anyone take care of details the way you do," Marcy said.

"Is that bad?"

"No, symptomatic."

"I don't want to leave anything to chance."

"The only thing—it leaves you so little time for other things."

"Like what?"

"You have to answer that," Marcy said.

"I'm solving problems as best I can."

"Do you think climbing is about winning?"

"Don't you?"

She smiled wistfully. "Poor Pratt," she said. "You just don't know."

To the northwest the clouds bubbled like a boiled sea. Tyms sat on a crag and ate chocolate. "It hasn't cleared," he said. "It isn't clearing."

"It will."

"It looks like a new front."

The sun warmed the rock they sat on, and snow was melting from the few places it had stuck on the vertical.

"We ought to move, then," Pratt said.

From the top of the chimney they kept right, dipped ten feet onto a spacious ledge, then started a sun-and-shade traverse that would take them to a long pitch toward the snowfield below the summit.

Tyms tested the conditions meticulously on the traverse. Pratt belayed. They climbed so often together Pratt knew what Tyms was thinking; he knew his moves. Tyms did not like the cold breeze swirling down from the crags.

A piece of frozen snow snapped off above, and when the snow hit rock, powder exploded over Tyms's head. Tyms was in the midst of securing a piton, and he swore. His goggles were around his neck instead of over his eyes, and the powder made the insides wet. To wipe them off, he unfastened his yellow hard hat. Just then another drift broke off. Tyms ducked, and the hat flew off his head, hit a rock, and bounced twenty feet out into thin air and disappeared below them.

"You okay?" Pratt called.

Tyms didn't turn. He moved upward, out of the shadow.

They finished the traverse and struggled with an icy overhang. Normally Tyms would have done the ice in a logical and precise way, but he was cold, and in hurrying, he made mistakes that cost them more time. Pratt kept silent.

Stay poised.

Calm.

Support.

The building clouds didn't help Tyms's frame of mind. He was right again: a new front was moving in, blocking the sun. Pratt was wrong. Water from the short melt froze into verglas; the snow turned crusty. Each movement took too many seconds, and seconds translated into minutes.

Tyms was visibly shaken when they reached the ascent to the snowfield. His face was red, the skin raw from the cold. He smiled, but the smile left quickly.

"We can head down," Pratt said.

"No," Tyms said. "It's a simple shot. We're fine. Up and off. That's the best way. We can descend the south face. That'll be easier than going back."

"But we'll save time . . ."

"Go."

Pratt made the free climb to the snowfield, belayed, pulled Tyms up the last few feet. "It's all snow to the top," Pratt said. "We won't stay long."

"Plenty of time."

"Just long enough to go over."

"It's one-twenty," Tyms said. "We should be up there by three."

"Two-thirty," Pratt said. "At two-thirty we go back."

He never got used to Marcy's way of thinking. Her beauty was not in her looks, but in the way she left him uncertain about himself, kept him guessing and on edge. She challenged him with a few small phrases which, days afterward, haunted him. She answered his questions with equivocation.

"Do you love me?" he'd asked her once.

"Yes and no."

"You came back from Chimborazo."

"What does that mean?"

"Well, coming back means you wanted to be here."

She replied with silence.

"Isn't that true?"

She stared out the cracked window. "What do you think about loneliness?" she asked.

"Is that what we're talking about?"

"Do you get lonely when you're alone?"

"I try not to think about it."

"Do you ever know?"

He'd tried to grasp what she meant, but she turned away from the window and kissed him.

Later he thought about loneliness without wishing to. Being lonely occurred to him when he was arranging a window display at the store, or when he emerged from the Buen Tiempo and glanced up at the mountains. Marcy never seemed lonely. She had friendly eyes and an enthusiasm to do many things. Yet why did she insist on being alone?

The last two hundred yards to the summit was a mindless exercise in pain. Pratt led, breaking the trail for Tyms. Most of the time the crust held, but when he broke through he sank into waist-deep powder. When Pratt tired, Tyms went ahead.

The snow consumed their energy. To their left the cornice angled sharply against the heavy gray clouds. The wind stiffened, and the windchill turned the air much colder.

Tyms did not lead for long; he tired quickly. That was a sign. In the lead again, Pratt slowed his pace. His feet were cold, and the wind bitter, and Tyms was silent. Tyms's usual step was gone. His eyes were haggard. Pratt stopped and gave Tyms his goggles, and Tyms didn't protest. He took them and put them on.

They persisted to the top. The view was not the familiar panorama Pratt knew from memory; no view of his house, no town buildings, no highways, no farms with alfalfa meadows, no wide sweep of other peaks. The clouds swirled around them, and the wind kept them low to the granite.

They shook hands and barely exchanged a glance. Then they went over and started down the south face.

"Relax, Pratt." Marcy kneaded his upper arm between her hands.

"I am relaxed."

"I can feel the tension. Your body isn't relaxed. You have to let the mind control the body."

"I am."

"You're not."

"If I'm not, how do I learn?"

She let his arm down and took hold of the other.

"You're old enough to know."

They moved more quickly on the broken trail down from the summit. They both knew the way. The snow cornice disappeared in the mist, and a gray airless space surrounded them. Off the windline they stopped.

"Shall we get something hot?" Pratt asked.

Tyms shook his head. "I'm all right. I'm cold, but so far it's just clouds."

Pratt nodded. It was not just clouds. The wind was stronger.

He led on toward an outcropping where Pratt knew in summer they had rappelled. The best way down was fast.

Tyms belayed while Pratt worked the traverse, but downclimbing took time. The wind made it more difficult. On the south there had been more melt, and now there was more ice. They had to use crampons the whole time.

Pratt let Tyms take his time. To press him was pointless. But Tyms moved like a sleepwalker. He felt his way along. On the rappel he didn't let go and catch himself, but rather slid along the rope a step at a time. He groped for footholds.

At the bottom of the first rappel, Tyms was exhausted. "Do you know the way?"

"Yes," Pratt said. "I know the way."

"I'm sorry about myself."

"Werner knows where we are."

"Not on the south side."

"He'll figure it out. Or Marcy will. We'll get down."

Tyms looked down the next drop. His eyes were yellow beneath the plastic of the goggles. "Forget Marcy," he said.

"Why should I forget her?"

Tyms didn't answer.

The storm hit in the middle of the next rappel. Wind, snow: a whiteout. Pratt couldn't see the rock beneath his feet. Tyms was somewhere below him in the snow, and Pratt yelled. "Keep on dropping. You're almost down."

Pratt thought he heard Tyms's voice in the wind, but he wasn't sure. He felt Tyms's weight on the rope. Not moving.

He fixed the belay, and then a piton to tie himself in. He slid off from where he was and descended.

Tyms was on a ledge, half conscious.

"We're almost there," Pratt said.

"No," Tyms said.

"I'm cold, too."

"It's not the cold," Tyms said.

Pratt felt Tyms's hands. Ice.

He braced Tyms against the rock and got out the Primus.

"Move before dark," Tyms said.

But the early dark had already begun, settling over them like another cloud. Light gray shifted to blue, then to deeper blue. The snow became invisible in the air.

The Primus blew out. Pratt started it again. He made Tyms put his hands over the pot of water. He made tea.

They finished the rappel. Tyms went first. Pratt knew exactly where they were. At the bottom of this cliff was a short ridge that petered out into an overhang. They would swing to the west and cross steep talus covered now with snow.

But they made bad time along the ridge. Tyms's steps were slow, teetering. Pratt held him. The snow let up for a few minutes, then came harder. The darkness folded in around them.

"Can you belay?" Pratt asked.

Tyms nodded.

"I'll use the light. When I get across this pitch, I'll fix a rope and come back for you."

Pratt shined the light into Tyms's eyes.

"Understand?"

Tyms nodded.

Pratt edged into snowy space. Using his ax, he moved in a rhythm of small steps, downward and outward. He drove one screw and moved. It was not that steep, and the wind had eased a little. The snow was heavy, though, and it was dark. In the beam of his miner's light, white slithered beneath him.

He did not panic. He worked smoothly, took deep even breaths, gauged his speed. When he had gone about halfway, he looked back along the yellow rope into the darkness.

"Tyms?"

No answer.

Pratt waited, then put some insurance into the rock.

Then without warning Pratt was jerked backward, straight out and away from the mountain. He held his ax with two hands, flailed in the air, bounced once, and fell.

The rope reached its length and wrenched him back. Tyms had got him.

Pratt bounced on the end of the rope, hit an icefall face-first, then scrambled to dig in with the ax. Somewhere, anywhere. He was alive.

"Tyms!"

He took a breath of air and snow. Twenty feet away he made out Tyms hanging free on the other end of the rope.

Marcy was so clinical. "It happens all the time," she said. "What difference does it make if you're hit by a train or fall off a mountain or die peacefully in your sleep?"

"It makes a difference to me," Pratt said.

"We're so small anyway. Compared to millennia, we've got only seconds. The difference between twenty-seven and eighty-seven is the blink of an eye."

"It's sixty years," Pratt said.

Marcy smiled.

"I know what you mean," Pratt said. "You're right, I guess. Unless . . ."

"No unless." Marcy paused a moment and gazed at him. "Oh," she said, "so you *believe?*"

Each small movement had to be protected. His shoulder and his right arm were almost useless. Small snowslides washed the cliff, and wisps of powder covered him. Going so slowly and carefully exhausted him. The cold was endless.

Pratt brushed away snow and drove two pitons in a crack with his left hand. It took ten minutes. He ran a short piece of security and tied himself on. He worked with a pocket light. He tested everything he did. Tyms's red parka was the only color he saw.

It took the better part of an hour to reach Tyms. Tyms was still alive. One of his gloves had come off, and his head was bloody beneath a knit cap. His legs were dangling. Tyms must have passed out and fallen headfirst, without a sound. The ice screw Pratt had set had held them both.

Sweat froze on Pratt's face. His legs were gone. He thought carefully: he could fasten Tyms to the mountain, take the extra rope for a long rappel . . . but to leave him there? And he was himself so tired.

He lit a flare, but the snow falling and the clouds kept the red light close.

He set himself on the ice, close by Tyms. Touching. To operate at sixty degrees suddenly became funny. His laughter was brittle and monstrous. Then anger: they had been stupid to go to the top. They should have turned back with Werner, or when they had seen the change in the weather, or when Tyms had first showed symptoms. Weak. His own training had made no difference. His anger diffused into the mountain. "Now," he shouted wildly to no one, "now, see?"

His anger vanished like a spirit into the cold. He bent his knees and knelt against the ice.

It was easy to love things in someone else you wished were in you. Marcy was so distant, so ready to disappear, but not afraid. He was afraid. He had always been afraid, but his fear was better than Marcy's lack. In love she was so silent he never knew where she was. She moved her lips in silent embrace, as if speaking, but to whom? She closed her eyes; she never looked at him. The closer he got, the more she backed away so he was forever guessing what she needed.

He wanted more than that.

He drifted. Cold seeped through his hands, his feet. Even the pain in his shoulder was numbed by the cold. The snow soothed him, danced white in the air.

When he woke, the stars had jumped into the sky. Orion was rising. Beneath him and far away, the blinking of the small lights of the town burned his eyes. He felt nothing in his hands and feet. His knees were frozen into the ice.

Werner's voice came from the edge of the ridge, almost in a whisper.

Pratt slid into and out of consciousness. Someone was chopping at the ice around his knees, someone was lifting him. He felt his body float free, gliding beneath the stars.

"Easy now, Pratt."

"Tyms?" Pratt asked.

"No pain."

Werner moistened Pratt's lips with water. The sky opened into a black space, bordered by a ridge of white. He breathed deeply. Cold. He was being lowered along the face of the mountain. He tried to say her name, but the word could not be spoken.

THE ACTRESS

ANDREA'S FIRST REACTION WAS ANNOYANCE: THE RED-BEARDED man would not leave her alone. He stood with his boot to her shoe, his large red head tilted downward like a crested heron's, staring as if in contemplation of her avoidance. He was dressed in baggy blue corduroy trousers and a sun-yellow shirt, and his expression was impish as Huck Finn's, or maybe, she thought, it wasn't so impish after all. She searched the gate waiting area for someone to rescue her, but no one noticed the man's strange behavior except her. "All right," he said at last, "you can stay at my place." He smiled at the right moment to cancel hard feelings.

"I have reservations," Andrea said as tightly as she could.

"Hey, I'm talking about *free rent*." The man's face grew redder, and his beard quivered. He sat down beside her in the molded plastic chair. "Name's Miles Himmel," he said, holding out his wide hand. "I'm going to help you out."

Andrea, by some mystery, found her hand in his, grasped firmly by thick sweaty fingers. "I think I'm settled," she said. "Thanks anyway."

"Off to ski, huh? The one-week deal?"

"Ten days."

"From?"

"St. Louis."

The man sucked air into his lungs. "A week isn't much time."

"Ten days," Andrea said. "No, it isn't much time, and I want to enjoy it."

"You've spent a bundle just getting to Denver, right? Then you have the package—supposedly clean condo, sauna, a hundred and forty bucks a night or more, bus service to the lift."

"Something like that. Actually, it's just a hotel reservation."

"How many times have you wasted money on that bullshit?"

Andrea frowned. She did not like the way this man spoke, even when he was right. She had wasted money before—at the Tetons one summer, and last year at Sun Valley. She'd saved for months. "This is my vacation," she said, and turned away.

"Look, my offer's genuine. People are sleeping on the windowsills in Telluride. At my place there are no conditions, no hours, no responsibilities. You can ski down to the gondola station." He straightened up in his chair and combed his beard with his stubby fingers. "All true," he said. "I swear."

Andrea softened a little. If he were serious, it would be a blessing, of course. Perhaps she would even be more relaxed if she spent less money. But he was a stranger. You didn't trust strangers, especially redheaded strangers. "What did you say your name was?"

"Himmel," he said. "You have to take some risks in life, or otherwise you miss out." He paused. "Call your friends. We can stop at the police station, if you want. They'll vouch for me." He smiled and paused again. "One other thing—I won't bother you."

Driving the icy road down from the Telluride airport in Miles Himmel's Jeep seemed less crazy than the idea of it had while they were waiting for the commuter plane in the Denver airport. The lights of the small town tucked in the narrow valley below them and the snow-covered ridges angling away, glinting in the clear air, seemed almost mystical. She'd done what she never would have done if she'd believed the newspapers. But she'd called a friend in St. Louis on Miles's credit card, and he'd supplied his driver's license and address and car registration. And there was something comforting, too, in his red hair and wild manner: he was recognizable. He could never do anything in secret.

Miles drove too fast on the curves, but he seemed in control, even when the Jeep slid to the outside.

"Nervous?" he asked. "I'll slow down."

"A little, but I assume you know the road."

"I've driven it a hundred times, and each time is the first." He slowed down as if to soothe her, and pointed through the windshield. "I live over there on that hill," he said. "See the gondola? Now isn't that better than any hotel?"

She had to admit it was. It was a palatial house, modern, wood with golden glass and a soaring roof. Beyond it the dim moonlight caught the mountains, illuminating dark patches of timber and the steep side canyons. The ski slopes were neat white fingers.

Miles turned left off the main highway, climbed a side road past condominiums and other huge houses. He stopped a mile up, shifted to four-wheel, and revved up a steep snowy driveway. The house materialized at the top of the hill, larger even than it had seemed from a distance—a gaudy, lighted bird hovering above the snow.

They leveled off and stopped beside a beaten-up red Volkswagen. "Ah," Miles said, "I'm glad Sheffield is here."

"Who is Sheffield?" Andrea suffered a stab of panic.

"No one to be afraid of," Miles said. He turned off the engine and smiled in the green dashlight. "Sheffield himself is not certain who he is. For a while he did odd jobs just to stay in town for the skiing. He's educated, brilliant in his own way." Miles snapped open the door, but sat for a moment. "I know one thing about him, though. He's never alone."

"He lives here?"

"Sometimes."

Miles got out and collected Andrea's big duffel and skis while she gazed at the house. It was a dazzling place, and she was suddenly elated she'd accepted his offer. At least she had courage still. Her paralegal job was tedious, and she'd lived the past year in the back-and-forth-to-work syndrome. So she wasn't *that* afraid to do something new. At the same time she was aware of all she didn't know.

She climbed the wooden stairs to the deck entrance where Miles had put her skis. He was waiting for her at the door. "Ready?" he asked.

"Ready."

He smiled easily. "Now, when you meet Sheffield, just play along."

Sheffield's skin was pewter in the firelight. With his arm jutting over the corner of the mantel, he gave the impression of a sophisticated man, slightly bored. He waved a greeting at Miles, and at this signal a woman lifted her head over the back of the sofa facing the fireplace. Right away Andrea felt embarrassed for intruding.

The woman had a model's thin face and arms, and rich dark brown eyes. "From Tulsa," Sheffield said, "this is Enid Lambert."

Andrea waited in the doorway while Miles went forward and shook hands politely. "Would anyone like a drink?" he asked. "Andrea?" He turned and looked at her.

She nodded.

"Bourbon all right?" He poured two drinks and handed one to her. "This is Andrea Sykes," he said. "Originally from

St. Louis, now from New York. We just met in the Denver airport." He smiled as if to assure her nothing would turn out badly.

"Miles was kind enough to offer . . ."

"A respite," Miles said. "Andrea's one of America's bright young actresses."

Sheffield and Enid Lambert both looked at her, and Andrea felt her face simmer. She was caught between making Miles look foolish and making herself look foolish. She chose to keep silent and do neither.

"So," Enid said, "someone famous?"

Miles's red beard twitched. "She's not famous yet," Miles said. "She's not the ordinary person who gets a quick break."

"What have you been in?" Sheffield asked. "Movies or plays?"

Andrea looked at Miles, who now looked quite serious. "You promised you wouldn't tell anyone," she said.

"Sheffield isn't anyone."

She glanced at Sheffield, then at Enid. "Plays," she said. "One movie, but it was a small role."

"What did you do in the movie?" Enid asked.

"I laughed." Andrea said, and she laughed nervously.

"For the whole time?"

"Once, in this one scene. It wasn't laughing, really. It was more like envy."

Miles crossed the room and went around the sofa. "Let me tell you about envy," he said cheerfully.

"You?" Sheffield said. "You don't envy anyone."

Miles shook his head. "You're wrong about that. As usual, you're wrong."

Andrea barely listened to the men's banter. She was desperately thinking what plays she had heard of or seen, how to fill in the blanks of the lie. Where in New York did she live? Did she know any real actors or actresses? What were the names of the theaters?

"Whom do you envy?" Enid asked Miles.

Miles looked at Andrea. "Her."

"But you've barely met her," Sheffield said.

"Yes, that's exactly it. Andrea can do anything she likes here. She's anonymous. And better yet, she's an actress. She can do any crazy thing without consequences. People will excuse her. Now if *I* started something—if I ranted in a bar or shouted on the sidewalk about Jesus or went around with loose women—people would say I'd gone berserk. They know me. But if she does that, it's normal. What do people expect of an actress?"

"I don't believe people would call you berserk," Sheffield said.

"Oh, yes, they would," Miles said. "But not her." He pointed at Andrea. "She's completely free."

The next morning, Andrea got up to a deserted house. She'd spent a restless night. Once she'd awakened with the bizarre idea of running naked through the streets in the middle of a snowstorm. Another time she imagined getting drunk and sleeping with two men at once. She even thought about shoplifting a pair of gloves. Who would know her if she were caught? Who would care in Telluride?

Then her excitement turned to a cold sweat. She wasn't the kind of person who'd do such things. She'd been dreaming. And besides, what if she were uncovered as a fraud? People like Sheffield and Enid would sneer at her.

But so what? She didn't know them.

Out the kitchen window, the sun fell across the valley onto a ridge of snow. She fixed herself eggs and toast. It was early still. The gondola hadn't started yet. A single blue car was suspended in her vision above the hill.

Perhaps she ought to check into a condo after all. She worried that Miles had some plan in mind for her, and she'd get into trouble. But she was not in trouble yet, and not miserable either. The night before, once the first blush of the lie had passed, she'd felt intoxicated with it. Sheffield had been witty, sarcastic, even tender toward her, and Enid was one of the most beautiful women she'd ever seen. Miles was the complete gentleman. She'd even wished he might flirt with her, but he hadn't, not once. He'd praised her instead, and the whole evening had been infused with brilliance.

She made her breakfast of bacon and eggs and Peet's coffee, and Miles came into the kitchen as she was cleaning up her dishes.

He poured himself a cup of coffee. "Good morning," he said. "How did you sleep?'

"Intermittently," she said. "Why did you say all that last night?"

"All what?"

"About my being an actress."

"People don't believe you even when you tell the truth," he said.

"But you didn't say the truth."

"You're Andrea Sykes, aren't you?" he asked.

"Yes."

"A name has no weight. An occupation—that's something else."

"You don't even know what I do."

Miles smiled. "You're an actress. Whatever it was you did before has been changed from a millstone to a helium-filled balloon."

He wished her good skiing and went down the hall.

She had a cup of coffee, too, and stood at the window. The

line of the horizon sliced upward through the blue sky, tree-less and snow covered, and when the line seemed most powerful, it stopped abruptly, and blowing snow feathered into the blue.

She skied to the Telski Office in Mountain Village, bought a ski pass, then rode lifts 4, 5, and 6 to the top of the mountain. The day was brilliant sun and blue sky, the snow dry and the trails perfectly manicured. She skied See Forever. Andrea was not the most elegant skier, but her body possessed a renewed energy important to her. She felt terrific. Her turns were tight, and she skied faster than she remembered from past years at Stowe or Taos. When she stopped and looked out over the expanse of snowy mountains, the heat rushed to her face, and she found herself laughing at nothing.

Several men noticed her when she rode the lifts up again. One of them was a rancher from Waco, Texas, about forty, nicely dressed. She liked his voice, and when he asked her to ski with him down Misty Maiden, she accepted. At the bottom of the hill, he asked her out for the evening. "I'd be most honored," he said.

"Are you married?" she asked.

"We'd just be having ourselves a good time," he said.

"I take that as a yes," she said. "And my answer is no."

She met another man in the lift line—a younger man in jeans from Salt Lake City. "What do you do?" he asked.

"Paralegal."

"Is that sort of like half a lawyer?"

"It's not . . ."

"Have you heard the one about the two lawyers in the john?"

"Fuck off," Andrea said.

She skied alone the rest of the afternoon and came down
the Telluride Trail at the end of the day with the zoo crowd.
Then she had a drink in town and took the gondola back up
to Mountain Village.

"Meet anyone?" Miles asked. He was standing on the
deck, holding something in his hand. He watched her walk
up the driveway.

"No one magnificent."

"How was the skiing?"

"Good, but tiring."

Miles waited for her at the top of the steps, and for a
moment, standing above her in that pose and with his eyes
in shadow, he looked menacing, as if he were laughing at her.
The object in his hand looked like a club. She mounted the
steps slowly, but when she reached the deck, he was relaxed
again, and gentle. "I have a date for you," he said, "if you
want to go out."

He unrolled the magazine he was holding, turned the
page open, and showed her. There was a color photograph of
a blond, sunburned man holding skis. A snowy mountain
rose behind him. The caption said he was Wyatt Clarkson,
PhD in English from Columbia, who'd come to Telluride to
hone his skills in the biathlon.

Andrea looked at Miles, who was facing the ridge fading
into shadow across the valley. "I told him you were an
actress from New York," Miles said. "You can go or not go.
Or you can tell him whatever you like."

Andrea glanced at the photograph again. The prospect of
going to the lodge or a bar and getting mugged by strangers
paled in her mind. And yet, when she went home, she'd
need some stories to tell. *What did you do at night?*

Miles's expression told her nothing. He was merely offering.

In St. Louis she'd have known how to proceed. She had friends whose tastes she knew. They fixed her up. Or she met men in her work circle, though all of them were paralegals or lawyers or judges. But what were her resources here? She knew only Miles.

"How open did you leave it?" she asked.

"Actually, it was Sheffield's idea," Miles said. "If you're interested you're to meet him at the Floradora."

On her way along the sidewalk, she window-shopped and watched the people. Some of the people watched her, too, and she felt clumsy, as if they were judging her. She hadn't been able to afford new ski clothes—the hotel was going to be so expensive, and St. Louis was not particularly a ski-clothes town. But with the money she saved staying at Miles's, why shouldn't she buy something to wear? Maybe nothing too exorbitant or daring, but something classy . . .

She went into Telluride Sports, and a clerk came over. "You have perfect eyes," the man said. "What can I do for you?"

A half hour later, she felt better. She'd bought pale blue stretch pants and a dark blue sweater. The town seemed to her more festive. Jeeps and four-wheel-drives moved along the snowy streets. The sidewalk was crowded. Everyone wanted to do everything quickly, as if the carnival might pull up stakes and leave town.

The Floradora was in the center of town, a saloon resurrected from the mining days. It was a little dark, but the crowd made up for the dim light. She found Sheffield at the bar.

"Been skiing?"

"Yes. You?"

Sheffield shook his head. "I live here," he said. "Would you like to sit at a table?"

They had the luck of openings and got a table by the window. Andrea felt self-conscious in her new clothes. The sweater was thin and tight, and she crossed her arms in front of her.

Sheffield ordered two bourbons before they sat down.

"How did you know I wanted a bourbon?" Andrea asked.

"If you didn't, I assume you'd have said. Or will you make a scene?"

"I usually don't drink much," Andrea said.

In the decompression of the night before, Andrea hadn't thought much about Sheffield. He had seemed funny, smart, good looking enough to attract a woman like Enid. But she remembered now what Miles had said. How was it he didn't know himself? He sat before her with a supercilious grin and blue eyes that were tired. He was not someone to fear.

"Where's Enid?" Andrea asked.

Sheffield shrugged. "I just met her yesterday."

"And you didn't like her?"

"She was all right in bed."

The waitress brought their drinks.

"Is that what you do here?" Andrea asked. "Test women in bed?"

"I don't have a job, if that's what you mean."

"You have money?"

Sheffield smiled. "I have Miles."

"The great philanthropist," Andrea said. "So tell me about Wyatt."

"Wyatt's a good-looking guy, smart. Are we finished with Miles?"

"I thought we were."

"What he seems to be he's not."

Andrea sipped her bourbon. "What does that mean?"

Sheffield sighed wistfully and looked across the room, as

if he were looking for a friend in the crowd. Then he turned
to her, and said softly, "What do you really do?"

Andrea felt herself blush, first in anger, then in embarrassed
relief. She checked the neighboring tables to see whether anyone else were watching her. "Was it that obvious?"

"Enid believed you," Sheffield said. "You did fine. It's just
that I know Miles."

"He told me to play along. I didn't know what to expect."

"You have a natural talent," Sheffield said. "If you want to
be an actress, be an actress."

Andrea stirred her drink. "I do and I don't. I'm really a
paralegal in a law firm. I feel like a para-person."

"What does it matter what you really do?" Sheffield
asked. "None of the adjectives we conjure up apply to anything real. Is a doctor really hard working and caring? I
assumed from last night you like to drink bourbon. Details
make us create lies, so what difference does it make if you
tell me or Wyatt you're an actress?"

"It makes a difference to me," Andrea said.

Sheffield drained his glass and called for another bourbon.
"So you like the lie of telling the truth? You okay with your
drink?"

Andrea nodded. "What do you know about Wyatt Clarkson?" she asked. "Miles said he was your idea."

"My idea knowing Miles." Sheffield smiled wearily.
"Wyatt's likable. If you want, I'll introduce you."

"I'd like that," Andrea said. "But will he believe me if I
tell him a lie?"

Sheffield shrugged. "If you believe it yourself," he said.

Sheffield and his date, Mae Jane Lovett from Charleston,
South Carolina, were sitting with Wyatt and Andrea in the
Fly Me To The Moon Saloon. Wyatt Clarkson was like no

man she'd ever met. He was not so perfect as his photograph
—his hair was not so neatly combed, nor his complexion so
smooth—but reality was better than perfection. His face had
movement, a twitch of the eye, a raised corner of the sleek
mouth, a smile in the dark eyes. He had traveled all over the
United States and Europe, had raced in Squaw Valley, Stowe,
Zermatt. After graduate school at Columbia, he had worked in
San Francisco as a house painter to grubstake his first year on
the biathlon tour. "I know it sounds odd," he said, "but at that
time in my life I would have done anything to train."

"It doesn't sound odd," Andrea said. "Doing what you
love is important. I find myself immersed and enchanted in
certain roles."

"Sheffield says you've been in the movies."

"Three movies, but only small parts. Jack Nicholson was
in one of them."

Andrea looked at Sheffield for his approval. He winked
surreptitiously.

"Did you sleep with him?" Mae Jane asked.

Andrea smiled an innocent smile. "I'm not telling," she
said.

They skipped from bar to bar. Drinks appeared before she
ordered them, and she scolded Sheffield. The strange thing
was she didn't feel a thing. The more she talked, the calmer
she was. She told anecdotes she made up about summer
stock or about the depressing days when she was out of
work. Wyatt listened carefully, and the more convinced she
was he believed her, the more she liked him. The more she
liked him, the wilder the stories became.

Toward midnight they were back in the Fly Me To The
Moon Saloon. She was talking to Mae Jane and asked suddenly, "How can you have a name like Mae Jane?"

"It's just my name," Mae Jane said. "In the South we

have names like that."

"Two names?" Andrea heard her own voice harden. "Bobbie Jo, Sara Lee." She giggled. "Mae Bea. Mae Bea not." She laughed and looked into the glittering chandeliers.

"You're drunk," Sheffield said.

"It's a mood," she said. "Actresses have moods."

Sheffield and Mae Jane disappeared around one in the morning, and Andrea was left alone with Wyatt. "I'm having such a good time," Andrea said. "I hate for this to end."

"It doesn't have to end, but we can go home."

"Let's have one more drink," Andrea said.

Wyatt was polite enough to agree.

Andrea ordered a double and drank it purposefully and quickly. When the bill was paid, she excused herself to be sick in the women's room.

Wyatt could not have been kinder. "It happens to all of us," he said, driving her to Miles's.

"I'm so sorry," she said. "I wanted to . . ."

"I hope I'll get to see you again," Wyatt said.

"Of course. I'd love that."

The next day her head ached, and she stayed in bed. She couldn't ski, though she could see through her window the sun was strong on the mountain. Toward noon, Miles tapped on her door. "Andrea?"

She feigned sleep. Miles opened the door and came in.

"Wyatt called," he said. "He asked whether you were still alive. I thought I'd check."

"I'm alive," she said.

"You had a good time?"

"Yes." She paused. "I didn't do anything terrible." She sat up slowly.

Miles stood in the doorway with a glass of water and an

Alka-Seltzer. "Apparently Wyatt enjoyed himself."

"Is that what he said?"

"And that you drank a lot."

"I can drink if I want," Andrea said.

"Of course you can."

An awkward silence rose in the room between them and created a crackle of electricity Andrea had not expected. The comfort she'd felt with Miles withered in his indifference. Miles walked to the window and looked out.

"Is Sheffield here?" she asked.

"I don't know. He didn't come home last night."

A moment passed.

"Do you enjoy this?" Andrea asked.

"What is that?"

"Our spectacle," she said.

Miles smiled at her, then dropped his gaze. "Wyatt wants you to call him when and if you want to."

She called Wyatt later that afternoon from the hall telephone.

"It was my fault," Wyatt said.

"How was anything your fault?" She heard her voice as angry. "I wanted to drink, and I chose to drink more."

"Let's forget about it then."

"Forget it? Why?" She watched her reflection in the hall mirror—the curve of her body invisible under her loose clothes, the hair to her shoulders as she'd worn it since college. "If I want to drink myself sick, I can and will," she said.

"All right."

"Do you understand me?"

"You can drink as much as you like," he said.

"Or do anything else I want."

"Yes."

"You still want to see me?"

"Why wouldn't I?"

Andrea thought of several reasons. "All right, then," she said.

That evening it clouded up. Banks of gray drifted over the mountains from the northwest and slid down over Ilium. Toward nightfall, the snow started, softly at first, then in great gauze sheets.

Andrea's mood lightened as soon as she saw Wyatt at the Floradora. They spoke in a superficial badinage she hadn't known she was capable of. She was more skillful at lying, more confident than she'd ever been in her life. She embellished parties she'd been to (one with Princess Di and Donald Trump), people she'd met (Tina Turner, Gabriel Byrne, Gary Hart). She invented stories that could never have been true about the old Andrea Sykes.

She did not drink much—just a glass of wine. Wyatt was the one who drank—one Heineken after another.

"When do you have to be back in New York?" he asked.

"When my agent calls."

"Days or weeks?"

"I've been reading a script. Joshua DeKalb is getting a cast together for a movie he's shooting in Montana. They know who I am and what I can do."

"What can you do?" Wyatt asked.

The clarity had left his eyes; his mouth loosened around the edges. She hesitated, as though wondering how to tell a secret, and looked around the crowded bar. There were other men as good looking as Wyatt or Sheffield, men whose stories she didn't know. Did they live here? She turned back and smiled. "I'd be a hitchhiker willing to kill."

Wyatt grinned. "Great! I can see it!"

"I may have to leave town soon."

"Not before tonight, though." Wyatt leaned forward.

"No," Andrea said. "Why don't we make dinner at your place?"

Wyatt ordered another Heineken and took it out under his coat.

They trekked arm in arm down Colorado through the snow. She loved the gray air, the brilliance of snow cascading through the street lamps, the touch of snow against her face. She put her head on his shoulder. "Will you ski one day with me?" she asked.

Wyatt reeled away from her and drank from his beer. He stopped on the sidewalk and studied a snowy blue Mercedes parked near the corner. Snow settled on his hair, his eyelashes. His expression turned bitter.

"What are you doing?" she asked.

Wyatt stared at the car. He walked around and tried the driver's door. It was locked. He brushed snow from the windshield and looked in. He went around to the grille and drank the rest of his beer.

Then he hurled the empty bottle as hard as he could into the windshield. The glass starred in front of the steering wheel: tiny white lines shot out from the point of impact. He turned and ran.

Andrea waited in the entry to Wyatt's condominium for an hour, watching the snow cut through the window lights across the street. She thought of calling Miles to find out if he knew where Wyatt might go, but she didn't want to talk to Miles. She didn't want a simple answer; she didn't want to cruise bars.

So she waited. Time slowed down. She thought how far away her office was, her girlfriends, the small apartment

near where her mother lived. The snow kept on hard, covering the streets, the cars, the trees, making the mountain
invisible.

Wyatt did not look at her when he passed. He brushed by
and unlocked the door, leaving it open for her to follow or
not. He didn't seem surprised to see her.

She closed the door quietly behind her. She turned on
the light and crossed the room to open the curtains.

"Leave the curtains closed," he said. "Turn off the light."

She turned off the light.

"I should tell you something," he said.

"You don't have to tell me anything," she said. She unbuttoned her blouse.

She moved closer, took her blouse off. It was simple to do
such a thing.

"I want to be honest," he said.

She unbuckled his belt, unbuttoned his jeans, kissed him.
She was an actress. She knew he was willing, and she had
done this many times before.

She woke up to Wyatt sleeping curled toward her with a
beer-swollen face and his hair sticking up every which way.
She smiled at this new image of him.

She got up and went to the bathroom, then came back and
stood naked at the window. She wanted him to see her. A
foot of snow had fallen outside, and people were shoveling
out their cars.

Wyatt stirred in the bed: she knew he was looking. She
tried to be casual about her body as she turned around.

Wyatt wasn't smiling as she thought he'd be. His expression wasn't admiring, but puzzled. "What is *that* look for?"
she asked.

"I've never slept with an actress before."

"Well, don't look at me that way."

"You're looked at all the time," Wyatt said.

"I've acted. I've *posed*. That's different."

Andrea reached for the sheet, but he pulled it away from her. She looked for her clothes, but they were in the living room. She was naked then, when before she hadn't been.

"Do you want to go skiing today?" he asked.

She tried to cover herself.

"Doesn't it look perfect out there?" he asked.

"You can see it does."

"I don't ski," he said.

"What do you mean? You said you'd go with me."

"I can't ski. I never said I'd go."

He handed her the sheet, and she drew it around her.

"Miles showed me the article about you in that magazine."

"I stood on some skis," Wyatt said. "Someone took a photograph. The writer made up a phony story."

"You didn't train for the biathlon?"

He shook his head.

"No PhD from Columbia?"

"My *name* isn't even Wyatt Clarkson," he said.

He reached for her hand.

"Don't," she said.

"Look, I wanted to tell you . . ."

She turned away. "Don't. Don't."

She found Miles in a small room under the eaves. He was sitting at an old IBM typewriter, a half-finished page rolled into the carriage. When she came in, he looked startled. His beard quivered, and he swiveled in his chair toward her. "You found out about Wyatt," he said.

"Wyatt told me the truth."

A wisp of a smile creased Miles's face. "Did you tell him about you?"

"No."

"Then you're safe."

"Safe?"

For a moment they looked at one another. Then she understood.

"You haven't been unhappy, have you?" Miles asked.

"No."

"Bored?"

"Not for a minute since I've been here."

"Haven't you been amused?"

The word was not right. Amused. She had been more than amused, more than entertained. Challenged. "You've made all this up," she said.

Miles smiled. "I gave you a place to stay," he said. "I left you alone."

Andrea was silent.

"Did I force you to do anything?"

"No." She whispered the word.

Miles swiveled back and faced his typewriter.

"But why?" Andrea asked.

Miles typed a few words.

"Sheffield, too?" Andrea said.

Miles lifted his shoulders in a sigh. "No one knows who Sheffield is," he said. "He's a graduate of Princeton. A skier . . ."

Andrea nodded. "I'm welcome to stay, then?"

Miles typed more words, then turned and smiled. "Of course. As long as you like. Oh, I know you have your job to get back to. But the summers here are cool. It rains in the afternoons. The mountains are beautiful. The meadows in the high country are green, such a brilliant green."

A FALSE ENCOUNTER

EVERYONE SYMPATHIZED WITH ADEN'S HARD REACTION TO HIS father's death. He and his father had been close, almost without rebellion on either side. One night Henry French skidded off a wet road, driving back from the South Shore toward Boston, a road his father should not have been on.

After the funeral, Aden spent a lot of hours playing solitaire, video games, watching television. Sometimes he scarcely moved for hours. His mother lived around the silence.

"Aden, you have to do something," she said. It was mid-morning, and he was watching a talk show.

"I am doing something."

"You're sitting."

"I'm doing something else besides sitting."

"You're not grieving," she said. "At least finish your thesis."

"I'm having second thoughts, third thoughts."

Everyone said it was not right, the silence. Then he started drinking. He showed up at family dinners and picnics with eccentric women gathered from clubs in Back Bay. The women wore all black, or leather, had rings in their cheeks and noses and eyebrows, shaved their heads or wore their hair spiked with colored wax. Among his family, sympathy turned to pity, then to disgust and rumor. He was taking drugs; he was sick. How could he turn against what his father had always boasted of as "his own people"?

His own people were the educated rich. In subtle ways he had been informed that he was in the line of succession—not that he had to perform any specific task, but he had to attain membership. And he was close. He had finished his third year of the PhD program in anthropology at Harvard when his father died.

He stalled. He could not bring himself to discuss foreign cultures, artifacts, theories of civilization. Struggles closer to home his father had championed—civil rights, The Nature Conservancy, eliminating poverty—seemed equally hollow, or luxuries he could not afford himself the pleasure of. There was no pleasure.

His mother's family was the weaker strain. Physically he resembled his father—high, sleek forehead, light blue eyes, dark brown hair a little thick, a strong, well-muscled body. But during prep school and college, he discovered his intellectual proclivities were softer, more suited to literature than to the pre-law curriculum his father favored. His father had a business veneer, fostered by an early career as a college boxer. Aden majored in English. Boxing had been dropped from collegiate athletics, and Aden tried rugby, then wrestling, and finally nothing.

In drinking, Aden was not so idle as he appeared. Alcohol focused attention inward and let him keep the basic mystery foremost in mind. He and his father had been honest with one another from Aden's earliest memory. Even his mother, who in summer preferred her family's place in the Berkshires to the company of her husband and son at the shore, had no understanding of the depth of their conversations. Father and son absorbed one another. They spent hours sailing in the bay, sparring with gloves on the wooden floor of the porch, running the dark sandy roads in the evenings. At night they drank and talked of the possibilities life offered—

not only for themselves, but for others. Service to society was part of the code of ethics of the educated rich. Each of them was required to make a positive contribution. In these long hours, they hid nothing, absolutely nothing. Genes made them close, and each knew the other as well as any man can know another. So Aden had thought.

The day after his father's death, the letter addressed to him had arrived in the mail. He had been home alone, his mother having gone to her sister's in Brookline. The postmark was Cohasset where the summer house was, the handwriting clearly his father's. But the letter was not in his father's voice.

> Dear Aden,
>   Three weeks ago I was sitting in my office think-ing of the past. I boxed a match once in college against a man much stronger than I, and for seven rounds I was getting badly beaten. There was noth-ing I could do. In the seventh I was hit hard and went down—I've never told you this—and as I was strug-gling to get up from the canvas, it occurred to me: why? Why should I rise valiantly and take more pun-ishment? I had already lost the bout. I did not have the strength to knock out my enemy. Continuing was pointless. Yet getting up was a reflex. It seemed then and now as what I imagine a dream to be. No one in a dream is ever capable of acting on his own.
>   Love,
>   Henry

Compared to his father's normal voice, the letter was unclear, almost mystical. Aden knew his father never had dreams and seldom spoke of memories, though Aden supposed he thought of them. Why had his father never told him this?

* * *

Aden asked the obvious questions about the accident. His father had been at the summer house all weekend and had no visitors that anyone had seen. He was driving the Porsche. It was September—Aden hadn't started back to school yet—and a cold drizzle was falling. It was dusk. His father had been driving too fast for the conditions, but not for the car. From the tire marks, the police judged his father had swerved to avoid hitting something. At seventy-five the car had veered sharply right and had crashed into a bridge abutment. He had been killed instantly.

The strangest thing to Aden was that his father had been on that road at all. No one knew he was going to Cohasset. In fact, Henry told his family he was flying to Philadelphia to negotiate a land-purchase contract for the firm. It might take some time, he said, maybe two weeks. He packed hiking boots.

And he called from Philadelphia. He spoke to his wife and then to Aden. Aden remembered his father's saying the city was terrible; he sounded tired, but not particularly distracted. "Tomorrow at least I can get out in some fresh air," he said.

There had never been a question in Aden's mind to keep his father's letter from the grave to himself. He read and reread the letter, considered its message, and decided his father's death was a suicide no one else need be privy to. The swerve off the highway had been intentional. He hadn't seen anything on the road: it had been a false encounter.

Again, why?

Aden made inquiries. He spent two days in November in Cohasset talking to the year-round people—one neighbor among the closed-up summer houses, the postmaster with white hair and white eyebrows, the caretaker Joshua Nordstrom. The neighbor, Mr. Lucas, hadn't even known his father was there. Josh Nordstrom hadn't been by, either, but the postmaster knew a little.

"Carrie Williams saw lights," the postmaster said. "The constable went out because the house doesn't have any heat."

"It has a fireplace."

"It was your father all right. Carson said he'd been drinking."

"How long was he here?"

"It was some days, I guess. We never delivered him any mail."

"Did he bring any in?"

"Maybe one or two letters."

"One was to me," Aden said. "Do you remember any others?"

The postmaster shook his head, looked at Aden askance. "I'm not a snoop," the postmaster said.

Carson Croft, the constable, said he'd found Henry French drunk as a college boy. "Up to him," Croft said. "I guess it was pretty cold out on the water."

"He wasn't drunk when he was killed," Aden said. "You notice anything else? Anyone with him?"

"No. I only went out that once."

Aden spent two nights in the house huddled in blankets on a mattress by the fire. His father had left a half-full bottle of Jack Daniels on the floor, and he drank enough of it to sleep fitfully. The sea wind knifed through the thin wooden walls and rattled the loose windows. He tried to relive what his father might have felt during his time there, but Aden felt distant. Who else might he have mailed a letter to?

When Aden got back to Boston, he called his father's secretary.

"No, the office didn't receive a letter after your father's death," Emma said.

"Did he go to Philadelphia?"

"I know the land deal went through."

"Who was the client?"

"Mr. Gates. He does a good bit of business in Boston."

"How long did the transaction take?"

"A couple of days. Your father wanted to attend to it himself."

"You made the plane reservations?"

"Yes. He took the limousine to the airport from here. His return was for ten days later."

"Why ten days, if the deal only took two?"

"I don't know. I think your father thought it would take longer."

He called USAir and found out his father had made the return connection.

Then he called Mr. Gates. Aden had never seen Mr. Gates, but his voice was harsh and gravelly, unsympathetic. He sounded displeased, as if he'd expected more of Henry French than two days' work. After the contract had been signed and delivered, Henry had more pressing business.

"But didn't you walk the property?" Aden asked.

"We never left the real-estate office," Mr. Gates said.

"Did my father say what he wanted to do, where he was going?"

"He gave me the impression he wasn't even here," Mr. Gates said. "He didn't tell me where he was going."

So there was a stretch of time—a week, perhaps a day longer—unaccounted for, before his father's bleak solitude in the summer house.

Aden's mother usually went to the Berkshires in late May, leaving Aden and his father to themselves to do man-things. That year was the first she was leaving Aden alone, and she worried about him. "You're welcome to come with me," she said. "It won't be like being with your father, but I'm good company. We can hike and play gin and drink it, too."

"I'll be all right," Aden said. "I may go to Cohasset. I may stay here. I don't know."

"But you'll be all right?" she asked.

"What do you think I'll do?"

"I can't predict what you'll do," she said. "That's what worries me."

The afternoon she left on the train for the mountains, Aden drove the family Buick to the shore.

He was surprised by his emotion when he drove through town. He'd been there recently, but it was a different season and a different time. A pall of disuse lay over the house, as usual, but now it had a feeling of loss. Grass had grown high in the yard and through the planks of the boxing platform; vines crawled up the clothesline poles. Inside, the rooms were dank from being boarded up all winter. Aden threw open the windows of every room and spent the morning in the hot sun mowing the lawn.

In the afternoon, he relaxed and looked out over the water. The diamond light of the sea burned his eyes. Toward three, the sky turned dark, and a breeze rose off the water. He shuttered the north-facing windows against a squall, and came back to the porch to watch the rain. His father had loved to be on the water in storms—those were the times he felt the test of his skill, not so much as a sailor, Aden thought, but as a survivor. He remembered his father at the tiller shouting orders, the sloop's heaving, the noise of water and the wind. Rain pelted the sea; the waves smacked the hull and arced over him at the mast where he reefed the main. His hands ached with cold; water raked across him, and he felt every minute as if the sea would sweep him away. The wind was a force beyond his ken. His father, though, never bent under the pressure. He ratcheted the main and kept the bow up into the wind.

It was only a few minutes since Aden returned to the porch when the clouds rushed quickly across the bay, and rain crackled at the metal drains. The storm burst around him. Rain flew into his face; the wind slid wooden chairs across the porch; a window cracked. Then in another minute the squall ebbed into a fine drizzle.

Later, at dusk, Aden fixed the broken window and built a fire in the fireplace. He sorted through the drawers and cupboards and bookcases, searching for what he didn't know. He came across decks of Bicycle playing cards, Scrabble, Boggle, sheets of music, novels he'd read. If nothing else, he wanted something to occupy his mind, a diversion. He tried a crossword in an expert book, played two hands of solitaire, read a magazine article that was ten years old. Then he found his father's college yearbooks in the kitchen.

The books had been Aden's first impression of Yale, sometime around age twelve. The stone buildings in the photographs, the suits and ties the students wore, the pomp and circumstance seemed to him from a dark age. Later, when he was in prep school at Exeter, the mannered poses of sports captains and the scenes from Mory's conjured ritual and serious intent that he came to admire. Yale, 1962–1965. Aden turned the brittle pages.

John Kennedy was president: there was a picture of him riding down Elm Street in an open Cadillac. The Cuban missile crisis was 1962. The Vietnam War deepened during those years. The Beatles were new. Drugs, protests, even riots marked the years. Students armed themselves.

Aden turned to his father's yearbook picture—long hair, a mustache and scraggly beard, bright dark eyes. Despite his father's facial hair, Aden was struck by the resemblance between them, even to the same crooked half smile. His father had long since shaved the beard and mustache, and for as long as Aden could remember his father wore his brown hair short. The eyes were the same, though in Aden's memory there were wrinkles around them.

But their bodies were different. His father had longer arms, therefore a longer reach. Aden's was shorter, squatter. Early on, of course, growing up boxing, Aden had adopted a quicker, defensive style to counter his father's long arms. He remembered crouching on the platform, swinging, jabbing, dancing, while his father held him at bay with a long left. Later, when he was grown, even though his father was slower, Aden had no offense, no punch to hurt.

It was then, looking at his father's college picture, that Aden thought of it—how his father frowned on living in the past. He didn't like photographs or histories. Aden remembered a conversation they'd had—was it at Christmas?—about the value of memory. "You have to consider the past to be able to plan the future," Aden said. "How can we know about tomorrow without being apprised of yesterday?"

"That's a fashionable thought," his father said, "perhaps even logical. I used to think that myself. But we have a history of assassination. How do you plan with that?"

"We understand peril exists. We protect ourselves . . ."

"But I mean we're wasting lives. We've become a nation of F. Scott Fitzgeralds and Beatlemaniacs, looking backward at good times."

His father protested recording anything—no tapes of TV shows, no receipts of bills paid, no photographs. The past was not evil, but memory should serve. So why had his father brought out his classbooks to the kitchen?

Aden remembered his father had one favorite picture, and he found it quickly. It was in the Senior History section, a paragraph about club boxing—it was not even a varsity sport—with the heading BOXING TAKES A DIVE. The sport was being eliminated from the university as too barbaric. The senior boxers were the last of a breed: Dacia, Appleton, French, and Freeman, dressed in dark Y-undershirts, holding determined expressions on their faces.

What had happened to these men? The thread of their relationships had been broken by his father's neglect of old friends. In recent years, his father had not kept in touch with people he did not see often. "What's the point of telling the same stories over and over?" his father asked once. "We all remember or we don't."

Yet his father, in the letter, had said he was sitting in his office thinking of the past. And he had kept the yearbooks. He mentioned a bout—what bout had he fought with what stronger man?

The next day, Aden called his father's office and asked Emma whether the office had a log of long-distance calls. "I'd like to know if my father called New Haven," Aden said. "Check the month of November of last year, before my father went to Philadelphia."

"I'll call you back," Emma said.

While Emma searched, Aden called information. A few minutes later, Emma called back. "There was a call to New Haven on November second," she said. "Twenty-eight minutes."

"And the number was 436-4771?"

"Area 203, yes," said Emma.

"Thanks."

Aden held down the receiver button, got the dial tone again, and dialed the number for the alumni office at Yale. "I'd like to get the addresses of some old family friends," he said to the woman who answered. "They went to Yale with my father."

* * *

Aden arrived in Lawrenceville, New Jersey, in the early
evening. He had driven straight from Cohasset in one spurt,
taking only what he had brought with him to the shore. He
knocked at the door of a white stucco. Frank Dacia was
watching the Phillies game broadcast from Chicago.

From the time of the college photograph, Dacia had
gained only five or six pounds from lightweight. His hair had
thinned, but the skin of his narrow face remained smooth as
a boy's. "My family will be back any minute," Dacia said,
turning off the TV.

"Then maybe I should ask you now," Aden said. "I'm
curious about what my father said when he was here."

"Isn't it strange how we find things out?" Dacia said,
shaking his head. "He was here only days before he died, but
I didn't read about his death until I saw the alumni reports
two months after it happened."

"I'm just learning about it myself," Aden said. "That's
why I've come down here."

"The *Yale Alumni Magazine* said it was an automobile
crash."

"That's right. He was doing seventy-five in his Porsche
when he was killed."

Dacia sat in his TV chair. Without the TV on, the room
came to rest on him, on his personal voice. "You know I'm a
prep school teacher," he said. "I've stayed in the yearly acad-
emic cycle, so I think a good deal about Yale. I go up for a
weekend game now and then. And I'm a committeeman for
reunions. I hadn't seen your father since we graduated. I
always sent him a handwritten note, you know—Henry,
how's the left?—but in that regard he was like Freeman. I told
your father this year was our thirty-fifth, but he shrugged. He
wasn't going. The past was too far behind him, he said. We
used to be pretty fair friends."

"He got to be like that," Aden said. "He didn't like dwelling on the past."

Frank Dacia was confused by this. "But we spent the whole evening he was here talking about the past," he said. "Your father maintained he never regretted anything—he said it two or three times. But in repeating it, he was less convincing. He dideth protest too much."

"We all regret some things," Aden said.

"I regret my college days couldn't last forever," Dacia said. "We were so close, though at the end things turned rather bitter. It wasn't a falling-out, exactly, but our senior year we could have done so much more. Your father did very well, of course. He trained harder than anyone else I ever saw then or since. He worked at weights, at the big bag, the small bag, and then after sparring he ran alone until it got dark. We might have won the intercollegiate club championship, too, if Freeman had competed."

"Why didn't he?" Aden asked.

"That's the curious part," Dacia said. He got up and paced, like a man suddenly turned old. "The night your father was here he drank quite a lot, and he talked incessantly about Freeman. Freeman this, Freeman that. I couldn't tell whether he hated the man or loved him."

"Do you know where Freeman is?" Aden asked. "He was the only one whose alumni record wasn't recent. There was not even an address."

"No one's heard from him in years. At reunions I heard he was selling his properties in St. Louis, but I don't know. That was from St. Louis friends."

The talk of Freeman spun Aden from his lethargy, and for the first time in months he was looking forward to the days ahead. He now had a mission. "I think my father found Freeman," Aden said. "Something made him commit suicide, and I know he talked to all three of you before he died."

* * *

"Of *course*, Henry French's son. You look exactly like him."

"People often say that."

"Talk like him, too." Dr. Richard Appleton pulled Aden inside the house with a friendly handshake. Had it not been for the similar styling of the gray hair, Aden wouldn't have recognized Dr. Appleton as the same man in the classbook photograph. He carried two hundred pounds, mostly toward the middle of a small frame. "Maybe you're a bit slighter than your father, right? Would you like a drink? I can't join you, I'm afraid. I'm off to do rounds at the hospital."

"That's all right."

They walked into the living room where a picture window looked out onto a wide terrace and, beyond it, a stable near some pine woods. A woman was working two geldings along a white board fence.

"That's my daughter, Ellen," Dr. Appleton said. "Florida isn't the best horse country—too damned hot—but Ellen likes the animals. Do you mind if she joins us? She admired your father."

"Fine with me," Aden said. "There are no secrets."

Dr. Appleton called on a pager phone, and Aden fixed himself a Scotch.

"She's coming right in," Dr. Appleton said. "I was sorry to hear about Henry. We expect some of our friends to die, but not your father. I thought he'd live forever."

"He was an athlete," Aden said. "It's hard to imagine an athlete's dying."

"Ellen and I had talked about him when he left here—how excited and enthusiastic he still was. I've slowed down to a leisurely pace, but your father hadn't changed from college."

Ellen came across the lawn and waved to them. She was tall and had long brown hair, and the sweat on her face shone in the sun. Before she'd entered the room Aden was on his feet.

"Ellen, this is Aden French," her father said. "You remember his father . . ."

"Of course I do," she said. She shook hands crisply. "It was a shock to hear he'd been killed."

"Killed himself," Aden said. "It was a shock to me, too."

"He knew how to live," Dr. Appleton said.

Aden was silent.

"I might have a bourbon," Ellen said. "You don't have to drink alone. My father was telling me about your father," she went on. "How heroic he was."

"In what way?" Aden looked at Dr. Appleton.

"Oh, there was one time I saw him knocked out—I mean, almost cold—and he got up again from sheer will."

"When was that?" Aden asked. "I know he lost his last bout against Harvard."

"Harvard was the club finals," Dr. Appleton said. "I'll bet your father never told you about the exhibition. He didn't like to admit failure, but this wasn't failure. It was a shame, really."

"Why was it a shame?"

"Your father thought himself invincible. But this exhibition, well, it was the worst match he ever fought. He was outpointed and outfought. . . . Something was eating at him, you know, the way the mind plays on an athlete. Ninety percent of any sport is mental."

"Who was he fighting?" Aden asked.

"That may have been it," Dr. Appleton said. "It was the time he fought Freeman."

"He never told me he fought Freeman," Aden said.

"They knew each other so well. They sparred together, trained together. It was an exhibition for a charity out on Whalley Avenue," Dr. Appleton said. "Your father fought

light-heavyweight, and Freeman fought middleweight, or
what's now called super middleweight, a hundred sixty-eight
pounds. Your father had the reach, too. But Freeman was
very strong. He had big shoulders, and if he had trained a little more, he'd have been professional material. Your father
was no slouch, either."

"I know that," Aden said. "He used to box me."

"I suppose there was a good deal of pride on both sides
since they were close friends. It appeared deadly serious,
though I couldn't see any anger between them. It was more
mutual respect. They fought even the first few rounds—
maybe your father had an edge in points. Then in the sev-
enth, Freeman landed a vicious hook. It was one of those
punches you can't make against a bad fighter, because only a
smart fighter like Henry would have leaned in at the precise
moment he did. Your father went down like a bolt.

"He rose to one knee at the count of four, then collapsed
again. Freeman had taken the corner and turned his back,
probably thinking he'd won, but I'll never forget his face. He
didn't look like a man who'd won. He looked dazed. He was
staring right at me—I was at ringside—but he didn't see a
thing."

Dr. Appleton stopped. "Then what happened?" Ellen asked.

"At nine, Aden's father was up again." Dr. Appleton turned
to Aden. "I don't know how he did it. Everyone knew he was
finished, but he got up. Freeman himself couldn't believe it.
He turned around and stared, and when the referee checked
Henry's gloves and let the fight go on, Freeman didn't move.
They danced a little. And then the bell sounded."

"So he recovered?" Aden asked.

Dr. Appleton shook his head. "Between rounds, your
father threw his towel into the ring. We all understood it.
He'd had enough. That one punch took its toll, and Henry

had made his point. He couldn't be knocked out. And why risk being hurt? It was a charity bout."

"And you think that affected him in the club championship?" Aden asked.

"I know it did."

"What about Freeman?" Ellen asked.

"Freeman won his next bout in a knockout in the first round, and he never boxed again."

Dr. Appleton looked at his watch and got on his sport jacket. "I'm sorry I have to get to the hospital."

"Boxing was eliminated that year, wasn't it?" Aden said. "That was the last bout."

"Yes, but the rest of us still sparred up at Payne-Whitney. We did some exhibitions. Freeman wouldn't have anything to do with us again. He didn't come around to the fraternity, and when you'd see him on the sidewalk, he wouldn't speak." Dr. Appleton shook Aden's hand. "I'm sorry, I'm already late. Ellen will offer you dinner. Spend the night if you like. There's a guest room upstairs."

Dr. Appleton left, and Aden and Ellen sat in the window seat, looking out on the horse pasture. They talked of horses for a while, Ellen's riding, the problems with the climate. Then they came back around to Aden's visit.

"You said your father killed himself," Ellen said. "My father read about it in the alumni magazine."

"He ran his Porsche off a rain-slick highway."

"Your father did come looking for Freeman," Ellen said, "but my father didn't know how to help him. He hadn't heard from Freeman in years. I'm sorry he's been no help."

"He told me about the exhibition," Aden said. "I know Freeman's from St. Louis. Frank Dacia said he had money. It shouldn't be too hard to find a man with money."

"My father has money," Ellen said. "You can do a lot of

things with money, and one of them is to disappear."

Aden stood up. "I'll let you know when I find him."

Aden gleaned an address for Scott Freeman through the Yale Club of St. Louis, though the club president, Sally Weymouth, said Freeman didn't live there. "His father was a member," Sally Weymouth said, "so we knew Scott was in the city for a while."

"How long ago?"

"It's been some years. He never came to meetings anyway. Scott was a recluse, even according to his father."

"And the father?"

"He died four years ago."

The address was in a fashionable downtown neighborhood, a walled fortress behind which brick mansions lived on quiet cul-de-sacs. The house had been recently painted, and an old gardener, not of the pickup truck generation, tended flowers beside the front porch. "I'm looking for Mr. Freeman," Aden said.

"You won't find him by looking," the gardener said. He did not glance up from troweling lupines.

"Does Mr. Freeman live here?"

"Mr. Winfield lives here," the gardener said.

"Who is Mr. Winfield?"

"He runs things." The gardener looked up. "I'll save you questions. He's around back."

Aden walked the flagstone path to the back of the house. He had spent an extra day with the Appletons in Palm Beach —with Ellen Appleton, actually, because he liked her candor. And she encouraged him to do what he had to do. "What else can you ever do that will matter half as much?" she asked.

Mr. Winfield was a young man, a little older than Aden, dressed in a coat and tie. He was sitting at a white-painted wrought-iron table. He'd just finished lunch and was drinking iced tea.

"The gardener said you talked to my father," Aden said.

"Your father was here. I can tell you that much."

"What did he say? How did he look?"

"How do you want him to look?"

"Did you tell him where Freeman is?"

"I don't know where Freeman is."

"Bullshit."

"I'm paid well to do very little," Winfield said. "I don't need to talk to you."

"Look, my father found Freeman. A few days later he killed himself. You must know something."

Mr. Winfield shook his head. "All I have is a postal box number in Denver. From the postmarks of what he sends me, he picks up the mail once a month, opens it at the post office or in the vicinity, signs and returns what he needs to, and takes the rest with him to send back the next month."

"You have no idea where he is."

"An important tax document came back once from Walsenburg, a hundred and fifty miles south, but he may travel constantly like a gypsy."

"So he could live anywhere," Aden said.

"He could be the Unabomber," Mr. Winfield said, "except they caught him."

The Buick hummed across the plains of Kansas. Aden's thoughts raced as quickly as the white road stripes under the car. He expected nothing, but he had to consider what might happen: what if he couldn't find Freeman? What if Freeman wouldn't speak to him? An entire life of uncertainty spread itself before him. The world wondered what happened to Amelia Earhart, how Jimmy Hoffa and Adolf Hitler had met their deaths, who was Anastasia, what became of Ambrose Bierce. Was that his father's purpose—to create a mystery around his death to keep himself alive?

An idea flickered in his mind. And then another—insane, frightening notions which, until that moment, had never come to him before. Appleton calling him Henry's son. *Talks like him, too.* Was he looking for Freeman in order to reach the same end as his father?

"You're so much like me," his father used to tell him. His father feinted a right hand, then delivered a long left. They were sparring on the wooden platform in Cohasset.

"I'm not you," Aden said. "I haven't got the reach."

"Of course you're not," his father said.

Aden feinted with the right and delivered the left.

Later that day, sailing a light wind in the bay, they'd talked about Yale. Aden had signed up for an undergraduate anthropology class. "If you have to delve into the past," his father said, "history gives you more of a feeling for the accomplishments of the species."

"But only of big events," Aden said, "or successful ones. Anthropology instructs you in how men have evolved, failed, and gone on."

"Nonsense. We don't deal with the world as a series of emotions. We formulate plans by rational processes, create a blueprint for our lives, and work to fulfill it."

"Is that what you've done?"

"Yes."

"And the goal is . . . ?"

"The goal is happiness. When you fulfill the plan, you've attained happiness."

The faint breeze lessened, and Aden caught the boom with his hand as it swung across the cockpit. "So there is no place for emotion?"

"I just said there was."

"You said there was happiness."

"Discipline," his father said. "History is a discipline. There's a direct connection between discipline and happiness."

"Happiness isn't emotion," Aden said. "And I'm not interested in events. I want to study the art and artifacts of societies that explain the emotions of a people as well as its way of life."

"You'll regret it if you do," his father said.

Eastern Colorado at sunset. The sun shone low from the plains. Barren ground. Pasture. Over the years his father had closed off more and more, retreated from his own history, and had seen only limited ways of being happy. A stranger to his wife. Looking back, it seemed to Aden his father could never have been happy.

Aden sat inside the cavernous post office in Denver watching the entrance and the rows of postal boxes. He hunched over a writing table and formulated his thoughts. He had the old college photograph before him. It shouldn't be difficult to recognize Freeman. Dark eyes, broad shoulders, curving arms could not change much over the years. Even though he might have days to wait, Aden sensed already a strange anticipation. Something was about to happen.

He was waiting for a man who had abandoned his friends, his house, his entire past, a man who had disappeared. Aden waited and watched and waited and read. Freeman didn't show up.

At day's end, Aden lay exhausted in a cheap hotel room and called Ellen Appleton and told her what he was doing and where he was.

The second day was like the first. Though he had spent days of boredom after his father died, he was not bored now.

He spent the third day waiting again, but instead of wearying, his senses grew sharper. Each succeeding day his anticipation notched higher. Freeman was closer to him than ever.

"I know he's coming tomorrow," Aden told Ellen on the phone.

"And what if he doesn't?"

"Then I'll wait another day."

"And what if he never comes?"

"Then he'll be like my father," Aden said.

Midafternoon on the eighth day Aden saw a gray-haired man in jeans and a blue collarless shirt walk into the post office. The carriage of the body in stride was graceful, but the face seemed older than the movement of the body. It was leathery and lined, and the dark, deep-set eyes were sadder than Aden had expected of one who'd chosen to live alone.

Aden half rose in his seat and then sat down again. Freeman opened his postal box and pulled out a stack of letters. He sorted these at the counter, throwing away some of them, setting aside the yellow cards for packages, putting other letters in a brown grocery bag. He took the bag to the counter and handed the clerk the yellow cards.

The clerk handed Freeman several packages. Freeman turned and walked in Aden's direction and glanced up. It was the moment Aden had been waiting for: the months of drinking, the days of uncertainty were over. It was no more than an instant. He had expected Freeman to notice him—*how much you look like your father*—but Freeman showed no trace of recognition. He walked right past Aden and out the door.

It was the instant Aden remembered. What if there were nothing Freeman could tell him? What if Freeman refused to say anything? As it was now, without speaking to Freeman, Aden could make up any ending. He could say his father had learned he had an incurable disease and had taken his life to avoid the pain of dying slowly. He could imagine his father had been severely depressed: the evidence was clear his father and mother didn't love each other. Perhaps there was an affair with an unknown woman that had broken off suddenly. Or a business reason: stocks had declined precipitously in the several weeks before his father had died. Was there some professional scandal about to come to light?

Or perhaps his father had never found Freeman.

Aden raced to the door and caught a glimpse of Freeman's blue shirt among the pedestrians. Freeman got into a small tan pickup truck. And still Aden could have called to Freeman. Even admitting his cowardice, he could have called. But he let Freeman get into his truck and turn into traffic in the busy street.

By the time Aden found the interstate, he was a good half hour behind. He pushed the Buick to ninety. Mountains stretched away to his right in distant shades and shadows of blue. To his left was the prairie. He drove south through the wide valley at Castle Rock, onward past the sprawl of Colorado Springs, where Pike's Peak with snow loomed over the whole city. In the cloudless dusk, an orange moon rose over the dry, flat plains.

He was not certain he was following Freeman. Freeman could have turned off the highway or headed in another direction altogether, but Winfield had mentioned Walsenburg, and Walsenburg was south of Pueblo.

At the post office it had taken him some moments to come to his senses. His own weakness kept him from talking to Freeman. He had been afraid. There was risk, yes, but what if he refused to endure it?

He had protected himself, had let himself believe his own

life hinged upon a single word or statement from a man he had never met. But how could it?

Somewhere beyond Pueblo, driving through a land of white moon, he came upon the small tan pickup truck—a Chevy. At the borders of the headlights, the country was desert, the mountains invisible, marked only by the absence of stars. Minutes and miles were of the same consequence. Guided now by the truck, Aden lost his own sense of direction. He was everywhere and nowhere.

Past Walsenburg, Freeman turned right onto a state road, then in a few minutes or miles onto another road, dirt now, leading through the same darkness. Freeman had to know he was being followed, but he didn't stop.

They climbed through aspen glades and into pines, and the air became cooler, clearer. Lights scattered far out on the plains. They curved up the flank of a hill and into dark timber.

Higher up, they emerged in a valley where Aden saw the arc light of a house. Freeman drove into the yard and turned off his headlights. Aden stopped a hundred feet behind, uncertain what he should do. He rolled down his window, ready with words. Freeman came toward him in the moonlight.

"I knew it was you in the post office," Freeman said. "Come inside, Aden. You're here about your father."

"You didn't let on you knew me."

"You sought me out. It was your place to speak."

Freeman opened the car door, and Aden got out into the cold night air. Stars were everywhere. They stood in silence for a moment, then Freeman led the way into the house.

The house was one room. A bed, two chairs, a stove, a table. In one corner, a desk covered with papers. Freeman kindled a fire and set a pot of water on the stove. Aden looked at the desk, which was the only place in the room that showed more than the bare minimum of life.

"My writing," Freeman said. He added nothing, and Aden asked nothing.

Freeman poured the hot water through the coffee grounds.

"I've retraced my father's life over the last several weeks before he died," Aden said. "It took me months to understand enough to begin looking."

"How did you know to look for us?"

"My father sent me a letter. I wanted to understand the words. It was in his handwriting, but it was as if it were written by a stranger."

"And what did the letter say?"

"He talked of memories and dreams and of a boxing match he never told me about."

"I got a letter from him, too," Freeman said, "but I didn't know he was dead." He handed Aden a cup of coffee, then went to the desk, where he pulled an envelope from among his things. "He was here for several days, and we spent some time walking in the mountains. I considered him serene."

He handed the envelope to Aden.

"Should I read it?"

Freeman shrugged, neither yes nor no. His expression was calm. "I assume it's what you came here for."

Aden opened the envelope and took out the letter. It was one sentence:

> Scott,
>   You knew, after all, for all the training, there was never any hope of winning.

"You know about the exhibition?" Freeman asked.

Aden nodded.

"I was the one who was helpless in that fight."

"But you'd knocked my father out."

"No, he got up. I suppose he meant to show me—to show himself—he could go on. But your father knew I could never hit him again."

"And that's why he threw in the towel?"

Freeman nodded. "Before he got up, before I turned around, I saw Appleton at ringside. He was on his feet, and *awed*— that's the best word for it. Stunned by what I'd done. Your father was an expert boxer, but I'd hit him very hard, harder than I thought was possible. I felt the blow as if I had received it instead of having delivered it. It jolted me, and I thought to myself, *I can't do this.*"

"But the next week . . ."

"I couldn't let them down. Everyone had trained so hard —as I had. We believed in what we were doing. If I hadn't boxed, I'd have made their hours and hours meaningless."

"So you fought one more round, and then you gave up," Aden said.

Freeman smiled briefly. "Call it what you want. I couldn't face people anymore. I couldn't hurt anyone else. Maybe it's insanity, but it's also a strength."

"What about my father?" Aden asked.

"Your father was the first person who had a reason to find me."

"I had a reason," Aden said.

"Your father had come to an ending in his life. That's how he phrased it. You were grown and on a course away from him. His wife, your mother, hadn't loved him in years. What he had believed in—happiness—was beyond him."

"But people cared about him. He did good works."

"He was like an animal that catches the scent of smoke," Freeman said. "When one is like that, even love is ineffectual."

"Then why did he come here?"

"He knew I would understand. But he wanted me to give him a reason to get up from that punch I had delivered years ago."

"And you couldn't give him one."

"I took him into the mountains with me. We climbed to a high lake with snow still melting into it. There were arnica and crimson staffweed blooming. The sun was warm, and we watched elk browse a meadow."

"I want to go," Aden said.

"Then I will take you, too," Freeman said.

The next day at dusk, Aden drove down from Freeman's cabin in the mountains. He had climbed with Freeman to the high lake and had sat with him many hours in the sun on an outcropping of granite. Around him was a stillness so pure he felt the light and the silence enter his body as if he were dreaming. There was no longer a need to speak, or to ask, or to answer. Freeman was serene and, after an hour, he had left Aden alone.

At Walsenburg, Aden stopped and called Ellen Appleton. He was all right, he said. He had found what he needed and was learning.

From Pueblo, he drove east through La Junta and Lamar out onto the plains. The sun retreated behind him, beyond the mountains, and the land ebbed to darkness. Aden felt the weight of time and sleeplessness, but he was at the same time alert and keening upon the light. He did not know where he was—on some empty road—when something rose up in the path of the car. He started in his seat, gazed at it, then felt a calm return to him. He bore down on the gas and kept the wheels of the Buick straight on along the highway.

DEATH VALLEY

VALERIE LEARNED LONG AGO TO FOCUS ON ONLY ONE THING AT A time, and just then it was piloting her Cessna 182 through the Panamint Mountains. She followed the thin gray highway over the mining settlement at Trona and angled now for the low spot to the left of Telescope Peak. The afternoon shadows crawled into the barren arroyos and over the ridges, and beyond the mountains she could see the sliver of Death Valley still in the sun.

Garabedian wasn't expecting her, and she was uneasy about sneaking up on him. Up till then he had been trustworthy. When she called him in the evenings, he was usually in his bungalow, and if his answering machine was on, he called her back soon after. He wrote her occasional letters, too, which was new to her—asking her advice on recipes or enclosing a magazine clipping he thought she'd like about golf. Still, she didn't believe his thoughtfulness was real. He was so often transfixed by clouds or by stars or by a warm wind that, when he was with her, she wasn't certain he was there. And when she tried to pin him down, he'd dance away on a joke or an ironic phrase.

Once they had made love at Zabriskie Point, on a rock ledge among the evening colors and shadows, and afterward she'd tried to get him to ask her to move in with him. She hadn't asked directly, of course, but she'd got her meaning across, and he'd stared at her as if he were surprised. "You don't like spiders," he said. "My house has eleven species of spiders."

Or maybe it was the way he made love that troubled her. No one else she'd been with had been so fierce and so gentle at the same time, and it unnerved her that he knew exactly what she wanted and when. How could she trust someone who made her feel so much light?

The Cessna buffeted a headwind and lurched forward. Val cut speed and sank down into the pass over the highway. On the other side, the land descended, ribboned by switchbacks, into the valley. It was October and still hot, and the foothills were bleached from the long summer. What animals endured there—snakes, lizards, a few desert bighorns—were hidden in shadow.

At Emigrant she turned northeast, away from the sun. Her ritual was to fly once over Scotty's Castle before she made her approach to Furnace Creek. Good luck, she called it. That was what she'd done the day she'd met Garabedian. He was delivering resort guests to their private planes, and she came into the airstrip too high and fast, and as if she had a last-minute change of heart, she flew through the runway and took off again. She drifted up over the golf course and came in with the right speed. Garabedian had waited to make certain she landed safely.

"I thought you were avoiding me," he said. "Are you all right? My name is Garabedian."

She skimmed the barren gullies and washes on the valley floor where only a few sprigs of mesquite and creosote gave a pale green hint to the tan and white. The mountains had no trees at all. They were jagged rifts of bare rock as high as any mountains in the country.

She circled Scotty's Castle, a monstrous monument to folly, and then turned southwest. Palm trees and the hazy green of the golf course feathered in the distance.

She wasn't expecting Garabedian to be with someone else, though imagining his doing to another woman what he did to her made her edgy. What she wanted was to see his expression when she surprised him. His face, not his words or the way he touched her, was his most reliable measure. She wanted to see whether he was glad or not glad, whether he embraced her right away or held back even slightly. That was the way she would tell if he loved her.

Val's father taught her to play golf when she was eight years old. There was a course across the street from their house in Ventura, and she played every afternoon after school and every day during the summers. She spent hours on the practice range, and in the evenings she putted by floodlight on a green her father had made in the backyard. Playing golf was what she wanted to do for as long as she could remember.

She won junior tournaments and the SoCal Amateur and was on the women's tour for two years and three months before she quit. Karrie Webb and Annika Sorenstam were the reigning stars, but Val was a comer. She was long and a little wild off the tee, but her play around the greens was solid. Her putting was exceptional, and week to week she learned to read the courses and to play without taking so many foolish risks.

She did well enough to buy a plane for travel between tournaments and a Lexus and a condominium in Santa Barbara. Then she had misgivings. She didn't know why. She hadn't fallen out of love with a man or argued with her father, who still coached her. If she could have named a physical reason— back spasms or pain in her wrists or a shoulder injury—she could have coped better. She just wasn't certain anymore what she wanted.

A psychiatrist gave her the impression her crisis wasn't serious. He'd prescribed Valium if she wanted to take it and said the pressure she felt would dissipate. She had enough money saved to get along for several years, so she moved back to Santa Barbara. For a while she practiced to keep her game together, but her heart wasn't in it. Then she flew her plane to different places where she could be alone. That was where she was going—nowhere—when she met Garabedian.

There were other men before Garabedian. That was how she knew how different he was. Other men never stirred her particularly. She had a boyfriend in high school, and Larry at the Lady Keystone, and another whose name she couldn't remember at the Westchester Classic. They were all too eager. She wanted to enjoy sex and did what she could to make it last, but always she was left adrift with nothing to say.

Garabedian knew something about her she didn't know about herself. The first night she was with him in his house she didn't know what to think. He wanted the doors and windows open. He wanted the lights on.

"People can see in," she said. "Don't you care about privacy?"

"I care about the circulation of air," he said. "I want to see you."

She wanted the dark. If she had to fake her feelings, she wanted the darkness to hide them in. And she wanted music, but there wasn't any. Then he kissed her. He'd touched her, and she forgot the lights were on, forgot feigning her desire. They made love in the living room standing up in front of the window that reflected their naked bodies.

Val set the Cessna down a little after five. She taxied to the tie-down area and fixed the wings with cables to grommets in the asphalt. She already decided she wouldn't call the inn for a ride. It was only a mile and a half's walk to Garabedian's, and the hottest part of the day was past. She left her clothes and her golf clubs in the plane.

The earth was bone-dry on both sides of the airport road,

and the asphalt radiated heat. A roadrunner scuttled between two clumps of mesquite and climbed a tamarisk stump along a dry ditch. A hundred yards farther on, Val turned off the pavement onto a service road and came out into a panorama of ponds and grass fairways and date palms.

The golf course was a little like Scotty's Castle—a monument to absurdity. Death Valley got only an inch and a half of rain a year, but the course was watered every night. Garabedian was the chief groundskeeper. He was too smart for the job, but he liked working outdoors. He liked the heat and the warm winds and the stars.

He said the water came from his own personal supply. "At night," he said, "I conjure up clouds from the mesquite and tamarisk and collect the moisture in the ditches and ponds. It's a form of magic. Would you like me to prove it?"

"Yes," she said.

That same night he led her out through the date palm grove. He walked quickly—he had on shoes, and she didn't—and in a few minutes he was far ahead of her in the dark. He ducked behind a palm tree where the grove ended and the fairway began, and she thought he was going to jump out and scare her. Instead, though, when she reached the edge of the grass, he was at some distance across the fairway, still moving away. She thought he looked like a silhouette in reverse—pale against a black background—and she called to him, but he didn't stop. She sprinted to catch up, but he disappeared over a ridge.

She felt lost then. The grass was soft underfoot, but the darkness stretched ahead. Her body tired quickly from running. Then Garabedian stepped from a sand trap, and she nearly collided with him. "There," he said, "look!"

She was dizzy, and her breath was ragged. She peered across the manicured green into the darkness. "Where?"

Only the wild stars were visible overhead, and the mountains were a serrated line where the stars left off. She moved closer to him to see what he saw, and when she touched his shoulder, she realized he was naked.

"You have to smell it," Garabedian said.

She kissed his bare shoulder. She smelled his skin, the grass, the scent of water. A minute later—how had it happened so fast?—she pushed him down onto the grass and lay over him, absorbing into her own flesh the smell of his body.

It was daylight now, though, as she walked across the fairway toward his bungalow. The mountains turned beige and pink in the fading light, and the arroyos were black with shadows. She took the cart path around the 10th green. Sometimes she missed the tour, but it was like missing a place like Ventura. She had grown up there. She knew the house and the configuration of rooms and the sound of traffic on the street. Even if she didn't want to remember it, it was there in her blood.

She crossed a bridge over a ditch and walked into the next fairway. A mower was running, and she paused behind a tree to make certain the driver wasn't Garabedian. She wanted to be closer to him to see his face.

Whoever it was idled the mower down and waved to her with his cap. It was Edgar Martinez, and Val waved back.

"Want to play tomorrow?" Edgar called.

"All right. Have you seen Garabedian?"

"He went to Barstow to get some irrigation pipe. How about noon?"

"Noon," Val called. "Come by and get me." She waved again, and Edgar revved the mower.

The fairway ran alongside the date palms at the back of the Ranch and Inn. It was the first time Val had seen date pickers there. Tall ladders were canted up against the trunks of the trees or braced in the beds of pickups. The men were high up in the fronds picking the dates, while the women and children emptied the baskets they lowered into boxes on the trucks.

Val turned down one of the empty rows toward Garabedian's. Migrants made her nervous. She saw them around Ventura and when she traveled the tournament circuit in the South, and she didn't understand how they could live without houses or plumbing or schools for their children. She didn't like the way they looked at her, either—the men or the women.

Until she felt them watching her, she hadn't been conscious of how she was dressed—shorts, a thin blouse, sandals. She was sturdy and tall and long-legged. Someone whistled at her, and she jumped to another row to get away from their stares.

Garabedian's house was on the margin of the grove. In the early days, before the ranch had become a resort, it had been the pasture for the borax company mules. Later when the mine closed, the houses had been moved to quarter the employees of the inn. Garabedian's bungalow was one of these—a one-story pink stucco with a front window that looked into the palms.

Garabedian's cocker spaniel, Joe, was barking in the fenced backyard when she came up. A migrant worker's car was parked in the yard next to the house, its doors open like wings, a baby asleep in the backseat on a piece of plywood arranged as a loft. A little way beyond, a boy poked a stick through the fence at Joe Cocker, and a woman said something to the boy in Spanish. The boy dropped the stick and came over to the campstove on the ground where the woman was spooning beans into a cup. Then the woman looked up and saw Val.

Val's face burned, and she turned away and went into the house.

Garabedian always left the door open. There were a couple of Budweiser cans on the coffee table on top of an open magazine, and dirty clothes were piled into one corner of the living room. She pulled the screen door closed and locked it.

She got herself a light beer from the refrigerator and rummaged to see what food she could find. There were carrots, lettuce, some grilled chicken wrapped in foil, and, in the freezer, three Lean Cuisines and two apple pies. She'd never seen Lean Cuisines in Garabedian's freezer before, and he didn't drink light beer.

She closed the refrigerator and glanced at the photograph held in place by a ladybug magnet. It was of Garabedian and his brother in Mazatlán with the marlin Garabedian had caught. The fish was hanging upside down by its tail, and the brothers had their arms around each other in that spirit of camaraderie men had. Garabedian's reddish blond hair was long, and he had a brilliant smile on his face—the smile she wanted from him when he saw her.

Joe Cocker jumped against the patio screen, and Val let him in to wriggle and crash around the kitchen. She filled his water bowl and gave him some kibble and put him back outside. Then she searched the house.

She sifted through Garabedian's dirty clothes, checked the empty pockets of his shorts and jeans, not looking for anything in particular, but for whatever was there. The bedroom was neater. He kept a stack of *Popular Mechanics* and *Golf Digest* (he read about golf courses, not golf) by the bed, but she found no pornography. There was nothing under the bed, either, except dust swirls and a dirty white sock.

On her way to the bathroom she glanced out the window at the car. The baby was crying, and the woman held the child on her hip while she ate beans from the pan. She was in her late teens or early twenties, and she stared into the distance as if she weren't seeing anything.

In the bathroom a half-dozen towels were draped over the shower door and on the towel racks. Val opened the plexiglas door to the stall, and a spider darted behind the paneling coming apart from the wall. The bottom of the shower had black hairs in it, and so did the sink—long black hairs stuck to the enamel. Val washed the sink with Comet.

What did she expect, for Christ's sake? She lived in Santa Barbara, and Garabedian lived in Death Valley. That was why he wanted it that way. She got another light beer and sat on the sofa. The magazine on the table was *Forbes,* opened to an article about art auctions in England.

II

That evening Edgar stopped by to see whether Val could play at ten o'clock instead of at noon. "If it's not too crowded, we could get in eighteen," he said.

"It'll be hot," Val said.

"Garabedian didn't get back?"

"Obviously not."

Edgar got a beer from the refrigerator. "Did you feed Joe?"

"Yes."

Edgar sat at the kitchen table. "I still can't believe you quit the tour. I guess you could get burnout, but it's always been a dream of mine—Lee Trevino, Chi Chi, Nancy Lopez . . ."

Val nodded. "There's a lot of politics, especially on the women's tour—women's golf versus the seniors', innuendos of lesbianism, the women's agenda for equal rights. How can we get equal rights without sponsors?"

"Is that why you quit?"

"No."

Edgar finally left around ten, and Val got undressed for bed. She wanted to be naked when Garabedian got home, but she thought of the pickers outside, so she put on one of Garabedian's T-shirts to sleep in. She dozed in bed for a while, then woke later to voices and laughter. The moon cut across the sheet and over her bare arms and illuminated the empty wall. The voices outside ebbed and flowed, and laughter boiled up intermittently. Finally she got up and looked out through the screen door.

A short distance away, under the palm trees, men and women sat drinking around a bonfire—maybe twenty of them altogether. One man got up and laid a dead palm frond on the fire, and the flames diminished for a few seconds before roaring up again even higher. She could see the faces in the circle, the delicate striations of the tree trunks, the undersides of the leafy palm fronds high up in the night. One of the men beside the fire was waving his arms and telling a story Val could not even imagine. She felt a chill hearing his voice, not understanding the language he spoke.

She got back into bed, and a few minutes later, a car door slammed beside the house, and Val heard scuffling. She peered out the side window. Moonlight shimmered from the roof of the migrants' car, and beyond it, a man stood urinating at the side of the road. The woman in the car shrilled at him, and he yelled back at her in a slurred voice.

After that Val couldn't sleep. She tried to think of Garabedian's touching her, his hands sliding over her skin, but outside the man and woman were arguing. Finally a child cried out, and the argument stopped. The man sang, and then the woman's voice joined his, and the child was quiet.

Val opened her eyes again when Joe Cocker squealed in the yard. Headlights swerved wildly across the bedroom ceiling, and Garabedian's truck skidded to a stop behind the house.

"Hello, Joe baby," Garabedian said. "Did you miss me?"

Val sat up and stripped off the T-shirt.

Garabedian came in through the kitchen and turned on the light. He got something from the refrigerator and took it into the living room. Val could see him through the doorway in the pale light from the kitchen. His shoulders sagged as if the hour were a weight. His stomach bulged a little. For a long moment he stared out into the dark date palms, and then, without turning, he said, "Hello, Val. When did you get here?"

"How did you know I was here?"

"I called Edgar around eleven and asked him to feed Joe."

Garabedian turned around, but the moment for seeing his face was past. He sat down on the sofa and pulled off his boots, then got up and turned off the kitchen light and came into the bedroom.

"What time is it?" Val asked.

"Four."

"You could have called me."

"I decided not to."

"Edgar said you went to Barstow to pick up some pipe."

"I went to Barstow, but it turned out the pipe was in Bakers-field." Garabedian said nothing more. He set the alarm. Change jingled out of his pockets when he took off his pants. He left his shirt on and lay down on the bed without touching her.

For a few minutes she waited. She wanted him to turn to her, to caress her shoulder, to kiss her. She wanted to touch his arm, his mouth. But he didn't move.

"Whose hair was that in the sink?" she asked.

Garabedian said nothing.

"God, please don't do that," Val said.

"I'm not doing anything."

"Light beer, Lean Cuisine, *Forbes* magazine." Her voice was too loud for the darkness.

Garabedian was silent for a moment. Then he said, "Since when did you start spying?"

Val heard the alarm go off and knew Garabedian had got up. After that she slept again and dreamed of catching a marlin. Garabedian was helping her land it, but the fish was too heavy in the water. Finally Garabedian swam out to the marlin and past it into the ocean until he was only a speck, barely visible. Then black gulls flew around her in the air. Their feathers were iridescent, and they made raucous noises. When she looked closely, they weren't gulls, but children nattering around her and flapping their wings in her eyes.

She woke again at nine-thirty with the sun streaming through the window. The car which had been parked outside the night before was gone. She cooked an egg and made toast, but she wasn't hungry. Edgar arrived a little before ten.

"He got back late, huh? He didn't look so good over at the shed."

"I didn't get much sleep, either."

Edgar smiled. "Is that good or bad?"

"Look, Edgar, I don't want to play golf."

"He spooked you that bad? What about nine holes? I've been looking forward to earning some money off you."

"Don't make me laugh."

"Golf is just what you need," Edgar said. "Come on, we'll go pick up your clubs. Five to one skins. You play from the men's tees."

Edgar drove his truck along the palm grove where the men were picking, past the guest cabins and the souvenir shops. At the highway he turned left in front of the restaurant. A little farther on Val recognized the car that had been parked at Garabedian's house. The woman had set up the plywood across two makeshift sawhorses and was selling sacks of dates to tourists. The little boy and the baby sat in the dusty shade of a tamarisk.

"She was at Garabedian's yesterday," Val said.

Edgar didn't look. "Garabedian lets some of the families with babies use his house."

"They take showers?" Val said.

"I guess so."

"Do they eat Lean Cuisine, too?"

Edgar smiled and shrugged his shoulders.

They turned west at the next intersection and accelerated on the straightaway toward the mountains. On the right was desert. On the left was the emerald grass and palm trees. Edgar drove straight ahead onto the airstrip to her plane.

Val climbed to the cockpit and got out a change of underwear and a clean shirt and stuffed them into her golf bag. Then she handed the bag and her golf shoes down to Edgar.

The bet was two dollars a hole for Edgar, ten dollars for Val because, as Edgar pointed out, she had a tour card and an airplane, and he had a ten-year-old Dodge truck. To avoid the paying guests, they started on the 10th hole, a 545-yard par 5 with thick brush bordering the drainage ditch on the right. Edgar lost the coin flip and teed off first.

He struck the ball cleanly and it soared down the center of the fairway. "I've been practicing," he said.

Val stepped forward and pressed her tee with the ball on it into the hard earth. She took some swings to limber up her back and thought of Garabedian. If he'd known she was there, why hadn't he let her know he'd be late? Had he really hauled irrigation pipe in the middle of the night? Or had there been a woman in Bakersfield? Maybe he'd only come back because he had to work.

She set her feet apart so the ball was a little to the right of her left instep. She took a deep breath and pulled the clubhead back slowly, rotated her shoulders, paused at the top of her swing. But she brought the clubhead down too quickly, and she knew as soon as she hit the ball she hadn't kept her elbow in. The ball tore through the air, hooked left, and bounded between the evenly spaced palm trees into the rough.

"Thinking of Garabedian?" Edgar asked.

Edgar won the first three holes, and they halved 13. He needled her on every hole. "Don't even think about the sand," he said once when she had to loft her ball over a trap in front of the green. "Isn't it pretty how they've put water over there?" he asked on another hole. And every shot he hit took forever. He looked up, looked down, bent his knees, moved his grip, looked up again at the flag. Once she'd yelled at him, "Come on, Edgar, hit the goddamn ball."

On the 14th tee he asked whether she wanted to double the bet. "I need the money," he said. "You can write it off as charity."

She was about to hit a seven-iron on the par 3.

"So what did Garabedian say when he got home?" Edgar asked.

"Shut up, Edgar."

"So four and twenty?"

"All right."

Val steadied herself. Her father had distracted her early in her career to toughen her up. He believed anyone could learn to concentrate. On rainy days he tested her with a deck of cards laid facedown to see whether she could match pairs, and when they drove to junior events, they played "I went to the store and bought bread, bananas, coffee, Alka-Seltzer, pizza, lettuce . . ." For a long time she attributed her success at golf to her ability to close away everything extraneous to striking the ball.

That was what she tried to do then, after Edgar taunted her. She closed out the idea of Garabedian, the irrigation pipe, the Lean Cuisine. She was about to hit, when she heard singing. It wasn't a radio, but real voices sifting out of the breeze.

She stepped back from the ball and looked toward the date palm grove. "What are they happy about?" she asked.

Edgar shook his head. "What makes you think they're happy?"

The voices stopped. The air was suddenly quiet, and Val felt an odd sorrow.

"It's lunchtime," Edgar said. "The Lean Cuisines were Garabedian's sister's. She's an art dealer in Phoenix."

Val came back with a birdie on the 15th and one skin, but she didn't care about the money. The 16th fairway adjoined the date palm grove where the workers were eating their lunches with their families. Garabedian was there, too, not eating, but talking to a man in a yellow hat and long trousers. A stack of white plastic pipe had been unloaded nearby next to a flatbed trailer.

Garabedian, as always, looked unkempt. He had on baggy shorts and a T-shirt and rubber boots because they were standing on swampy ground.

Val hit first off the tee, and to avoid the swamp and Garabedian, she moved her stance right. She struck the ball with a solid *thwack,* and it scooted down the fairway grass and across onto a maintenance road that led to a shed behind the tamarisk trees.

"Trouble," Edgar said.

"You want to make some real money?" Val asked. "What about fifty dollars and four hundred dollars?"

Edgar smiled. "You think money will psyche me out? All right. We'll do it."

He teed his ball and did his heron imitation—bent his

knees, looked up, looked down, up again—and drove his ball left into the date palms.

"Trouble," Val said.

She took a sand wedge and a nine-iron from her bag on the cart and started across the fairway. Edgar drove the cart over toward Garabedian.

Her ball had stopped in a shallow depression on the service road. If she had hit it a few feet left or right, it would have rolled into the ditch, but as it was, she had a decent lie. The ball was on loose dirt, and she had a clear line to the flag between a tamarisk on the right and a solitary date palm in the fairway. She opted for the nine-iron.

Edgar called to her to hit first. He hadn't found his ball yet.

Val addressed her shot, gauged how far the flag was, looked down at the white ball. Then a hawk's shadow passed over the road in front of her. She watched it slide along the ditch and break apart in the brush and coalesce again on the bare earth. A hundred yards down the ditch, the shadow veered left and vanished, but something else caught her eye where the birds's shadow had disappeared. It looked like someone lying face-down in the reeds and shallow water—someone in a tan shirt.

Val was sure it wasn't a person, but whatever it was didn't move. She looked over at Edgar, who waved her on.

She settled in her stance again and took a deep breath. She knew it was a person. The clubhead rose into the air. She was conscious of keeping her left arm at her side, of the clubshaft's making an L with her arms at the top of its arc. She hesitated a split second, then shifted her weight forward. Metal struck earth and ball, and the ball skied into the air. Val didn't watch it. She stared along the ditch where the reeds obscured the man's body.

Her ball landed on the green a few feet from the flag.

* * *

Park rangers pulled the body from the ditch and hosed it down. They covered the man with a sheet and took him to Barstow. The pickers called him El Tejon, the badger. No one knew where he had come from. He had hitchhiked to Death Valley and kept to himself, they said. Sometimes he slept under a bush on the golf course. He was solitary. Sometimes he showed up for work, and sometimes he didn't, so no one had gone to look for him.

But the night before he had been at the bonfire. He had drunk too much and had told a story about a beautiful young girl in Mexico who was blind. She loved the man, and he sent her his money. The girl might have been his wife or his daughter. No one had been sure. Perhaps El Tejon had made up parts of the story.

That afternoon Val washed down a couple of Valium with orange juice and took a shower against the heat. Afterward she stood in Garabedian's living room with a towel around her and watched the pickers in the grove. They were high in the trees putting dates into the baskets cradled with ropes from the ladders. Women and children on the ground emptied the baskets and collected the dates which had fallen randomly from the trees.

Val was at the window when Garabedian came home. He quieted Joe Cocker and put him in the yard, and then he got a glass of water and came into the living room.

"Are you all right?" he asked.

"I'm afraid," Val said.

Garabedian stood behind her and put his arms around her waist.

"Don't," she said. "Please."

Garabedian took his hands away. "You must be as tired as I am," he said.

She watched the pickers balance themselves on the ladders without using their hands, as if the dates they picked kept them from falling. Shadows in the grove melted into one another, darkened the whole air. How could she explain how tired she was? She couldn't tell Garabedian, but if she didn't tell him, how could he know?

"I'm going home," she said. "There's nothing else to do now."

"You can stay if you want," Garabedian said. "Wait a few days. If you're upset . . ."

"No, I understand now. I need to go." She turned away from the window. "I'm sorry."

"Me too."

She got her clean clothes from her golf bag and went into the bathroom to put on her underwear and her shirt, her shorts and sandals. She hung the towel on the door with the other ones.

"When you can, come back sometime," Garabedian said. "Call me."

"I'm leaving my golf clubs," Val said. "Can you give them to Edgar? He can sell them. Or maybe he knows someone who can use them." She paused. "Tell him not to practice so hard."

A few of the pickers had started singing in the trees. Their voices were soft, barely audible from the house, and were joined by the women's voices on the ground. Val pushed open the screen and went outside. It was still hot. She walked out into the date palm grove and down the lane where the pickers were singing, toward the green fairway that opened in front of the mountains.

THE TENNIS PLAYER

A SIMPLE MOTION MADE FROM THE SHOULDER. HIS LEFT HAND holding the ball came to the left knee, and as the weight of his body shifted forward over the baseline, Nicky's arm swung upward in an arc. Suddenly the tennis ball appeared against the blue sky like a moon rising. Through years of practice, countless tosses, Nicky saw only the ball. It hung there poised, and in the precise moment before it fell, the crack of the racquet sent it away.

Nicky forced himself halfway to the net, but he lunged more than ran. Agee sliced the ball back. It came high and long, and Nicky paused a split second to decide whether it would go out. It had been too long since he'd last played to know by instinct. His hesitation was the choice: he let the ball sail. It struck the court just beyond the baseline, out.

He turned a moment in Agee's direction, smiled at luck, and walked back to the fence where the ball had stopped rolling. His smile faded. With a familiar motion, he dribbled the ball effortlessly from the court onto his racquet. With that simple retrieving, no stranger could have told he'd been away. He tossed the ball lightly from his racquet face to his left hand and stepped to the baseline left of center.

When he was younger, twelve and thirteen, Nicky had had tantrums on the court when the ball wouldn't go where he wanted it to, when he couldn't make it do as he wished.

He cried when an opponent cheated him. He remembered that well. He read the lines honestly himself, and he couldn't keep others' falseness from bothering him. A couple of times, when he lost on cheating, he broke his racquet on the ground, but it was only out of love for the game. That's how he explained it to his father.

"You can work out a new racquet at the store," his father said.

"But he cheated," Nicky said. "I would have won."

"Two hours a day," his father said. "You can still play tournaments on weekends."

His father was a photographer, a face freezer. Nicky moved lights into position for sittings. He knew what to do—eliminate shadows, let the face show itself so it could tell the truth. What Nicky learned early on was the camera: how the lens worked, the way an image was reversed on the plate, how to brush away imperfections in a print. And he knew the chemicals—developers, toners, fixers, rinses. He memorized the flaws his father took away from the faces of women and children, newlyweds, business executives who returned to the store to collect their own images.

The ball hung in the air, and Nicky served into the tape. The second ball he topspinned, and it turned oval on its flight over the net, thudded in the service court, and bounced high and away to Agee's backhand. The return was angled to Nicky's left, and he reached out awkwardly, out of position for the skidding underspin. The ball skipped by him, and he stopped short. Without expression, he turned and walked back again to the baseline. Agee lobbed a second ball over.

Nicky thought of his father's saying the King of Sweden had played tennis into his eighties. Nicky's own movements were slow and dreamlike, as if he were so old. He had told himself not to expect too much, but the last ball was hittable, a shot he should have played easily.

He remembered Agee differently, too. When they had played before, he was slower, more cheerful. Now his friend was distant, uncertain, a tougher competitor. Why had Agee lured him out to play?

Or perhaps it was Caroline. "We all imagine what you've been through," she said. "We know it wasn't easy."

They were sitting on the swing on the terrace behind her house in the warm spring night. Before, they had often sat there: a favorite place. The terrace overlooked a long wide swath of lawn which extended down to the dark trees.

"We try to understand as best we can," she said. "All of us. But Nicky, you can't close us out. You have to try, too. You have to try to come back to us."

He'd closed his eyes then. And how did one go about coming back? Yes, he wanted to come back. There was nothing he wished for more than that, to have everything just as it was. But happier. He had been so tired then.

"Can you tell me?" she asked.

He'd searched for words. "It's as if no one else has moved," he said. "And I've moved a great distance."

"But that's not true," she said.

"Suppose I decide to do only one thing—a job—for the rest of my life," he said. "What happens then?"

"Then you become something." She moved closer to him on the swing and set it moving with her feet. "At least then, if you make a decision like that, you've started to move."

"And what if the one thing you decide to do turns out to be without value?"

Caroline stopped the movement of the swing. Inside, the telephone rang. He thought she was angry at his saying such a thing, but as she turned to look at him, he saw in her eyes she did not understand. She never thought that way. Hers was a world of application, restraint, respect for property. She had no sense of emptiness.

She didn't answer his question. Instead she leaned toward him and kissed his lips.

Then her mother came to the terrace door. "Nicky, it's Agee on the phone."

"He wants you to play tennis," Caroline said. "Tell him you will."

"I don't want to." He stood up from the swing.

"That's what I mean, Nicky. You have to try to come back to us."

Now the first time was over. Nicky zipped his racquet cover on his Prince while Agee rounded up the two cans of tennis balls. Nicky had one in his hand.

"You can see the shape of the old self," Agee said.

"Nearly extinct," Nicky said.

He put the ball into the can Agee held out, and they headed for the clubhouse.

"Later in the summer we'll play tournaments again," Agee said.

Nicky remembered the summer before, when they'd toured the state like circus sideshow performers playing in front of the crowds. People cheered errors, jeered at them for winning.

"No tournaments," Nicky said. "That's over."

Nicky stopped on the path, seeing Caroline coming toward them. She looked bright and breezy, her blond hair against the green trees. She twirled a daisy nervously in her fingers.

Everything at the club looked perfect to him—the spacious lawn, the trees, the clubhouse with the blue-and-white-striped awnings. It was the rest of the world that was imperfect.

"I watched from the dining room," Caroline said. "You both played very well."

"I thought you weren't going to be here," Nicky said.

She took his hand and looked at Agee. "He'll be playing as well as ever, won't he?"

"It won't take long," Agee said. "Really."

Really. They were both being enthusiastic precisely because they weren't sure. He felt like an invalid who had to be walked and talked.

They said to him, "Nicky, look at the light."

He looked at the light. He was sure he had looked at the light. It was a small point. The voice came from their skulls, not from their mouths.

"Nicky, look at the light."

The voices echoed as if they were in a cavern.

He was sure he looked at the light, but they kept repeating it.

Caroline led the way into the clubhouse, and Nicky and Agee followed. She was at home there, at ease. "I've ordered lunch for us," she said. "I hope that's all right."

The interior of the clubhouse was lavish. The entry, coatroom, and hallways were done in red cloth brocade; a wide, air-conditioned clubroom led to windows overlooking the golf course; the reading area had soft leather chairs, glass tables, magazines of all kinds. Nicky stopped. Seeing the magazines startled him. Before, before he went away, he had stopped reading newspapers and watching television and looking at magazines. That was the first sign.

At the entrance to the dining room, Mr. Davidson, the club chairman, came over and shook hands. "Good to see you back, Nicky," he said.

Nicky nodded. It was as if he were back from the war, except if he were back from a war, their welcome would not have been so guarded.

Mr. Davidson held on to his hand like an old uncle. "Looked pretty good out there, I must say."

"Thanks," Nicky said. "I wish it felt good."

"Look at the light."

The light came from a point in the flashlight. He looked at it.

"That's fine, Nicky."

In the beginning he'd seen the light, but then, as they said "fine," he had not. He couldn't move.

"Look at the light again. Over here."

He moved his head, but didn't see anything.

"That's very good, Nicky. You're getting much better."

Caroline moved off with Agee, and Mr. Davidson drew Nicky aside. "I have a favor to ask you," Mr. Davidson said. "Maybe it would help you out, too."

"Sure," Nicky said.

"The club pro—you know Jerry—can't give lessons in July. He has that clinic up in the Adirondacks. We could use someone to fill in for a while."

Caroline and Agee took a table at the window. The dining room was white tablecloths, silverware, glasses that caught shards of light. The window looked out onto the green world.

She looked over at him as if she knew the conversation he was having, knew what Mr. Davidson was asking. She nodded, and her mouth moved in pantomime. Say yes, she said.

"Look at the light now, Nicky," they said.

"It looks different," he said.

It was still a point of light, but he smiled when he saw it. The light was very clear and still.

"You're going to be home pretty soon."

"I know," Nicky said.

"Have you made any plans?"

"Not really, no. I thought I'd stay around home and rest."

"What about tennis?"

"Maybe play a little tennis again," he said. "I don't want to rush into anything."

"Thirty dollars an hour," Mr. Davidson said. "Plus half the proceeds of the pro shop."

"I haven't played at all," Nicky said. "Just today."

"But you haven't forgotten how," Mr. Davidson said. "It's like riding a bicycle. And it's only lessons."

Nicky still looked at Caroline. She was talking to Agee, the light from the window in her face. She was intelligent and beautiful and knew what she wanted. Tennis used to be spending days in the sun.

"I'm sort of at loose ends," Nicky said. "I could use a job. You're right. It would help me out."

"Good," Mr. Davidson said. "Then we're all set. I'll tell Jerry."

He was on the court at eight every morning in sneakers, white shorts, a short-sleeved shirt, sunblock. The sun burned him. In slow motion he demonstrated the strokes of the game to children and ladies: forehand with the handshake grip, reach toward the net with the follow-through. It was better to learn the traditional stroke before working toward the heavy topspin the pros used. Backhand: pull the shoulder back, coil it, then step and release. Lock the elbow at the moment of impact. The serve was like throwing the racquet across the net without letting go. Timing. The toss and the racquet had to reach the same point in the air at the same time.

He watched the awkward legs and arms of the women, the tentative bashful swings of the girls, the wild, uncontrolled hitting of the boys. He listened to them laugh at their own mistakes, or laugh in their frustration. "This isn't easy," he said.

From the moment he agreed to teach, Nicky began a new

relationship to the people around him. He gave in to telling people what they wanted to hear. Of course, in the details of the senses he was scrupulously honest. He didn't charge people too much for tennis socks. He gave an hour of his time for an hour's lesson. When a shot was in, he called it in; when it was out, it was out.

But he did not tell everything. He said the truth, but not what would hurt.

"I don't mind the work," he told Caroline.

"Really, Nicky?"

"Really."

He didn't mind the sun, or the standing up all day, or the people. But he hated the sounds, the repetition, the enclosed space with the fence and the green windscreen around it, the gate to get in and out.

Sometimes Caroline met him for lunch. They sat in the snack bar where moments of his former life were hung on the walls: his arm around Agee when they won the state doubles title; another of himself holding the sectionals trophy; the time he'd qualified for the U.S. Open. His smile in those photographs was genuine.

"You ought to think about tournaments again," she said.

"Maybe I will," he said. "What are you doing tonight?"

"My parents are going out," she said. "Would you like to come over?"

"What time?" he asked.

At two he met a class of boys eight to ten. Caroline watched. She sat beyond the fence on a bench, laughing at the way the children moved and hit and ran after the tennis balls. He devoted his time to teaching control. "You can't hit a tennis ball as hard as you can in any direction," he said. "You have to remember there is a net to get the ball over and lines on the court. It does no good to slug the ball. Place it. Hit it where the other person isn't."

The ball machine tossed them ball after ball to a perfect spot. "Watch it," Nicky said. "Racquet back sooner. It's too late when the ball is already there. Prepare. Now step in when you swing. Gently."

Caroline was his only respite, but she was the danger, too. He spent most evenings with her. They went to movies sometimes, to plays in the city. Most often they sat out on her terrace, talking idly. He did not tell her he loved her. She believed it without words, and he let her. And at times he did love her, but since it was only at times, he knew he didn't.

They made love sometimes when her parents were out. They walked down the lawn to the edge of the dark trees, spread out a blanket, and undressed on the grass. All else faded from his mind then, even the terrible light. He knew she wanted no other than him, and she believed he wanted no other than her.

Yet the truth was he wanted no one. Even as she lay beside him, as his hands caressed her and hers moved over his back, as his desire rose, he did not think of her. It was not her fault; and he did not *not* want her. He did not want anything. She moved over him, pressed her body into his. He saw her pale face against the dark trees and the stars. He wanted this: not thinking. Lovemaking was the end of thinking, all attention drawn out of himself. He wanted the lovemaking to last forever, and knowing it wouldn't was his anguish. Knowing he would wake and be asked to speak was a grief he knew he must endure. Feeling such a thing was the worst he could do; he knew this, too. Yet it was all he could do and all he had before his body gave way and he found the world pale and less tenable than ever.

Always the next day he was back on the court with the women and children. He varied his method—some days serves first, some days talks on strategy or rules—but the variation was within a framework, within the lines of the court, the game itself.

Sometimes his mind wandered to the hospital where he had been separate from all of them, beyond their visions, away from all else, the all-else unknowing it was to blame. His mother used to say to him, "Nicky, are you well? You don't look well." But what did looks have to do with it?

He went to the photography studio and helped his father. He understood his expression was the equal of any of the posers, that he was removing the flaws from his own face as he was removing theirs. Day to day he moved along a tight-rope, the fear of falling increasing as the height increased, as the rope became looser: the cars television taxes directions space flights schedules discussions airplanes motels computers money neon swimming pools success government medicines advertisements driving him forward over the loose rope.

He stood in one spot on the court, leaned over his basket of tennis balls, picked out eight at once. "Careful now, watch. Follow through. Keep your eyes open."

July was made of the same weather: hot days, blue sky that opened outward and beyond. His skin baked to a deep tan; his hair lightened. Jerry pleaded with him to keep on: he wanted to stay in the Adirondacks where it was cooler. Nicky accepted. "I'd be glad to," he said.

Nicky never believed himself what he knew others inferred. He watched himself too closely to make his words out to be otherwise. He drifted, not bothering to explain.

He labored through the first weeks of August. The routine required no thinking. But the days became long, each one an eternity. He added each day to the ones before, and each day he thought he would fall.

Caroline said, "You look so much healthier being out in the sun. You're so much more like your old self."

"I am myself," he said.

"Look at the light."

He saw the point of light, but he could not move.

"Do you think you might try a tournament?" she asked. "A small one."

"I think I might," he said. "We'll wait and see."

Toward the end of the month, he often told Caroline he was delayed at the club and couldn't come over to her house till late. This was true, but not for the reasons he knew she would believe. She thought he had a late lesson, or he had to keep up with the accounting of the pro shop, or he had a meeting with Davidson about maintenance of the courts. He couldn't leave, though, because he wanted to be alone.

The club was the perfect place. In the evening the courts were no longer sprayed with tennis balls; he did not have to watch the children race after errant shots; he did not have to say anything polite, or anything at all. He stayed because of the absence. The golf course was empty. The green world closed around him, and the air was filled with the sounds of crickets and breeze in the leaves. He liked the dark.

One evening he stayed later than usual. He lay on the strip of grass between the tennis courts and the golf course and stared at the sky. He stared through the sky, watching the blue darken to violet. The trees wavered across the fairway. Stars began. He imagined how deep the sky was, how the sky beyond the layer of ozone was pure space. The loose tightrope hung over that space. He wished the fall would be peaceful, as serene as looking.

The world moved through several hours just looking.

Then a motor hummed and headlights turned from the quiet pavement to the clubhouse onto the gravel drive behind the tennis courts. The lights scattered in the leaves above him. He sat up, and the headlights swept across his white clothes. In the shadow behind the headlights he recognized the car as Caroline's Saab.

The car door opened and closed. "Nicky?"

He didn't answer; she saw where he was. She had on a pale dress, colorless in the dark. A ghost coming toward him. He lay back again and stared at the sky.

"I thought you were going home tonight."

"I said my mother asked me to come."

"But you didn't go. I called over there. We thought something might have happened."

"Nothing happened. I've been lying here on the grass."

She folded her dress under her and sat down. "When you weren't there, I was worried," she said. "I wanted to see you."

Her voice was new. Nicky turned on his side toward her. The sun from the day still burned in his skin. He reached out and touched her arm, as if he could postpone with lovemaking what she had to say.

"I talked to Agee," she said. "He wants to know whether you'll play doubles with him in New York."

"Why doesn't he talk to me?"

"He's not sure about you," she said. "He's afraid to ask."

"We haven't practiced," Nicky said. "We haven't played."

"It's not for three weeks."

"I have my lessons," he said.

"But you're a top player, Nicky. You don't want to go on giving lessons forever."

He turned away from her and looked up. All he could think of was falling through the endless dark space.

"Nicky, please."

"Okay," he said.

Space. She leaned down and put her head on his shoulder,

moved her body beside his. She took his hand and pulled it toward her, pressed it to her breast. She touched his cheek, slid her fingers to his lips. "Oh, Nicky," she said. "I'm so glad."

Nicky hit with Agee for an hour and a half every morning, and Caroline signed up for an hour's lesson every afternoon and gave the time to Agee so they could hit for another hour at the end of the day. Agee was good for him. He made Nicky move. He hit the ball hard. He challenged.

"I can't," Nicky said over and over. But he could. He felt it. The mistakes diminished. He watched the ball better, concentrated. He did out of instinct what he belabored in lessons: racquet preparation, little steps, use the body. In two weeks the legs were more elastic, he moved well to the ball, he anticipated where Agee would hit. His serve improved from fifty percent to seventy, and it had more pace. He whittled his ground strokes deeper into the court, closer to the sidelines.

Caroline noticed, too. "You must see the improvement day to day," she said. "You must be thrilled."

"I notice," he said.

"I see the improvement," Agee said. "I don't think you were away, and the lessons haven't hurt you. You're stronger than you were."

Nicky smiled. He knew the quickness was returning. His serve felt solid, his ground strokes more reliable. He had begun trying shots that had been dormant a year and a half—the short topspin crosscourts from both sides, the backhand volley down the line, the big second serve instead of the safe kicker.

Even his mood during lessons was improved. He wasn't bored. "Weight forward," he said. "Never step backward. Keep moving."

Only one thing held him back: Caroline.

Every day she was there, not pressing him really, but there. She stayed close to him, but she was wary, as if he had lied to her. "Tell me the truth, now, Nicky," she said. "What are you doing tonight?"

"I am telling the truth."

"You're not planning anything?"

"No. I'm not planning anything. Did you think the other night was planned?"

"Yes."

"I wanted to be alone," he said. "When I'm alone I'm not lying to anyone."

"You don't have to explain," she said. "I understand. Do you think I don't want to be alone sometimes, too?"

"It wasn't you," he said.

"Now look here at the light, Nicky. Over here."

The point of light was very far away. The voices came from space. He tried to move, but couldn't.

"So you're back, Nicky. What happened out there? Look at the light."

"And now you think your life has purpose?" Caroline asked. "You've decided that one thing?"

"You said yourself I had to make a decision."

"But tennis, Nicky?"

She began to weep for no reason, but he knew reasons were not visible. She put her arms around him and held on tightly.

Before every tournament match in the old days, Nicky had had a ritual. He sat by himself for half an hour in some quiet place and concentrated. He held his fists closed for a minute at a time, pounding them slowly and soundlessly against his knees. He told himself to watch the ball, to hit hard no matter what, to relax. He told himself if he got behind to change his strategy: think. Think. Before each serve, bounce the ball three times for luck. It couldn't hurt. And if he were winning, never think he'd won until the last point was played.

The hour before the tournament in New York, Nicky knew he was not in the old days. He went off by himself, but he did not think of watching the ball, or bouncing the ball three times for luck, or about what to do if he were behind or ahead. He thought about Caroline.

He had been with her the night before. They had been sitting quietly, she on the swing and he on the steps nearby. He looked down the lawn to the dark trees and listened to the crickets.

"Come sit with me," she said.

He had not moved. He sensed in her voice she meant to tell him what troubled her, what she knew. "What do you have to tell me?" he asked.

"Sit with me first," she said.

He had got up from the step and sat on the swing beside her. The swing was still. She had her feet on the bricks. She took his hand.

Then with a suddenness he hadn't expected, the words burst from her—a child, Nicky, a child—and for a long time he sat there holding her hand, listening to her breathing in the dark. He was aware of himself growing dimmer and dimmer, and he'd been afraid. He stood up and walked down the lawn.

They made love by the dark trees, and he told her he loved her. It was not any kind of omission, but a lie. He had to say it. He could not bear the dishonesty, but he had to say it.

"Look at the light now, Nicky."

He did not see a light.

"What was it, Nicky?"

He didn't move.

"The light is over here. What was it? What happened?"

He was silent. He could not speak. Space closed around him.

"Was it the lies, Nicky?"

He did not see anything.

He took his racquets out to the court. In the warm-up, he hit the ball as if he were concentrating. He knew his opponent from years before, and Nicky was certain to win easily. He moved around the court, reacting without thinking. He hit his practice serves crisply, like the old Nicky.

Nicky won the toss and stepped to the line, right of center. He bounced the ball three times for luck, leaned back and pointed the racquet toward the net. A simple motion from the shoulder. His left hand holding the ball came to the left knee, and as the weight of his body shifted forward over the baseline, Nicky's arm swung upward in an arc. Suddenly the tennis ball appeared against the sky like a moon rising. Years of practice and countless tosses had taught him, but now the ball disappeared before his eyes, and all he saw was the wide, deep expanse of space.

FLOATING

WADE PLANNED FOR THEM TO STAY IN A MOTEL IN POCATELLO before going on to float the Middle Fork of the Salmon. It was late afternoon, and there was still plenty of light over the dry hills to drive another hour. But when the idea of the motel came up, Terry found a pine tree symbol on the map. "It looks like a state park," Terry said. "Why can't we sleep there?"

"If we drive farther today, we'll get to the river earlier tomorrow, and maybe we can get in some fishing."

"There's a lake," Terry said, looking at the map. "Why do we always do what you want?"

Terry was fourteen, and Wade didn't want the boy to think he had no input, especially when Wade didn't get to see him that often anymore. They were partners, friends. That's how Wade wanted to think of it. He didn't want Terry saying later he'd been forced to do something against his will. They turned off the interstate and drove east.

It had been a year since Dana left Galveston and moved with Terry to Houston. Dana said she needed to gain confidence in herself, and at first Wade thought the separation would be temporary, like an illness they'd get over. They didn't talk of divorce, but they didn't discuss reconciliation, either. Wade kept on with the printing business his father had started in Galveston. What else could he do? But the margin was small. Speedy-print outlets based on computers made it tough to compete, and Wade's plant was old. But he was skillful at design, and he put out calendars, announcements, chapbooks, flyers. For a few months he drove back and forth to Houston to see Terry on weekends, but when nothing changed with Dana, he went every other week, and then once a month. Even a fool got weary of the pain of not being loved.

The map said the road was paved, but after a mile, at the sign for Devil's Creek 17, the asphalt petered out into gravel washboard. Even in the Pathfinder, Wade had to slow down to a crawl.

Seventeen miles took them forever, and when they arrived, the sun was low over the yellow hills. The campground was not a state park, but a nearly deserted unimproved recreation area with a few seedy trailers at the shallow end of a drawn-down reservoir.

"There's a knoll across the lake," Terry said. "That'll be good."

"I don't think we can camp there."

"Sure we can. Nobody's there. Why not?"

The basin of the reservoir was about two miles long from the dam to where the creek fed in, but there were forty vertical feet of exposed mudflats and barren, striated shore. At most, the water itself was a mile long and a half mile wide. They drove over the dam, and Wade gunned the motor of the Pathfinder up a steep hill to the top of the knoll.

The knoll would have been an island if the reservoir were full. It was pretty flat, covered with sagebrush and grama grass, and he and Terry rolled out the tent in a soft spot. Wade threaded the aluminum poles into their sleeves, while Terry wrestled out the cooler and the Coleman stove from under their coats in the backseat. Then across the water, they heard children shouting. Wade couldn't make out the words. He paused and listened and finally decided they were speaking another language.

That was when he noticed all the fishermen. He finished the pole he was working on and then got out his binoculars. The fishermen were Indians. Their faces in the circle of the glass were stolid and angry, Wade thought. Bitter. The men sat at the edge of the reservoir, drinking beer and looking out where their fishing lines disappeared into the pale blue water. The children played with sticks and chased each other, while higher up on the hard sand, the women huddled around clunker cars.

Wade pointed across the water. "Maybe we should go to the motel after all."

Terry looked to see what Wade saw.

"When it gets dark, they might massacre us," Wade said.

"Oh, come on, Dad. Don't be paranoid."

"I am paranoid."

The tent was a red caddis fly, big enough for three, though not with room to stand. Wade stretched the fabric over the poles and knocked in the first stake with the back of an axhead. Terry pulled out the camp table and set it up. Then he got out his basketball and dribbled around the tent and the car.

Terry had driven Wade crazy in the car. He sat in the backseat and twirled the ball on his fingertip and passed it from hand to hand. When he bounced it off the windows, Wade forbade him to play with it in the car, but to compensate, he agreed to stop in small towns—Lampassas, Childress, Springfield—so Terry could have his basketball fix. He was a point guard: he dribbled and passed. All they needed was a parking lot, though now and then they found a netless hoop in a park. Even then, Terry wouldn't shoot.

"What if other teams find out you can't hit the open jumper?" Wade asked.

"I fake and hit the cutter."

"Doesn't it help your team if you score?"

Terry shrugged. "I don't have a team."

Now he dribbled through the sagebrush, alternating left and right hands. He dribbled halfway down the hill and back up again. He dribbled the ball between his legs. The sound of the bouncing ball, Wade knew, reached across the lake.

"Why don't you take a swim?" Wade asked.

Terry caught the ball. "The water looks cold."

"You could read," Wade said. "You've been putting off your summer reading. Or you could help me."

Terry dribbled some more. He dribbled behind his back. He dribbled low to the ground. He could dribble. Wade had to admit Terry could dribble as well as anyone his age, even on unlevel terrain. It was almost like floating, it seemed so natural.

Most of the fishing rods were untended, propped in piles of rocks or between slingshot Vs stabbed into the sand in front of a camp chair, and now their owners drank in small groups. A few fishermen braced themselves and flung their weighted spinners out into the deep water.

Wade put down the binoculars and opened the cooler for some ice.

"Uh, oh," Terry said.

Wade thought he was referring to the gin and tonic he was making, but why shouldn't he have a drink? The camp was set up, the rain flap stretched over the tent, the sleeping bags and pads inside, the lantern ready. But when he glanced up, he saw the basketball had hit a stone. It caromed down the hill toward the water.

Terry gave chase, but the ball was round and had gravity as an advantage, and it splatted hard on the water. With its momentum, it slid on the smooth surface out of Terry's reach.

"A steal," Wade said. He scraped ice into his glass and poured gin. "Looks like you'll have to swim after all."

Terry looked up and gave Wade the finger, and Wade realized Terry would never swim now. Terry followed the basketball along the shore. Wade smiled and cut the lime he'd stored in the cooler in a plastic bag.

The drive from Houston had been exhausting and hard work. When he planned the visit, Wade thought Terry would want to windsurf in the Gulf or fish for bass or go to Six Flags, but instead he wanted to climb mountains in Colorado and float rivers in Idaho.

"Why do you want to do that?" Wade asked.

"Because Texas is hot and flat."

"People freeze at high altitudes," Wade said. "They pass out from thin air."

"Come on, Dad. . . ."

As usual, it was Terry's voice that made Wade give in, the way he made Wade sound like a scared old man. They climbed the West Spanish Peak near Walsenburg and then Pike's Peak—14,110 feet of sheer agony. Wade's feet blistered and his lungs ached, and his legs were gone. Afterward he spent two days recovering beside a motel swimming pool while Terry dribbled his basketball incessantly.

The only respite Wade had from the basketball was looking up a woman he'd known in college. She was his lab partner in biology and later the class fund-raiser. He talked to her occasionally on the telephone.

"So who's the friend?" Terry asked when Wade was getting ready.

"Someone I knew at Rice. I don't have to go if you're nervous."

"Dad, I'll be fine. Mom goes out."

"She does? With whom?"

"I don't know."

"Why don't you know?"

"I stay at Grandma's."

The thought of Dana's going out with someone else and telling that someone about him made him nervous. And the idea of the man hearing her stories, learning her laughter, discovering her body made him sick at heart.

"Can I really watch any movie?" Terry asked.

"MTV is not a movie."

"Okay, okay."

"You can watch sports, too."

He met Katie Mitchell at the Edelweiss for dinner. She had aged well, he thought. Her blond hair was shorter, but her skin was nearly unlined. Her figure was trim and her fashion impeccable. "Money helps," she said.

She was tougher than he remembered her—she'd been divorced for five years—and she drank more than he did. After dinner, when she kissed him in the parking lot, he was surprised not so much by the kiss as by the urgency of it. He hadn't kissed a woman other than Dana in seventeen years.

"I have the perfect terrace for a nightcap," she said. "Will you follow me home?"

Her house was in the foothills, and the terrace was what she had promised. The lights of the city flowed east to the dark plains, and the clusters of stars were brighter than he'd ever seen. They had cognac outside.

"We're closer to the stars here," Katie said. "Don't they let you imagine the wildest places?"

"They make me feel small," Wade said.

"Only if you let them. They could just as easily make you feel as big as the sky." She unbuttoned her blouse and held the corners in her hands and twirled in a circle so that the white material looked like wings.

Wade put down his cognac. He saw what would happen next if he let it. "I think I should get back to Terry," he said.

The sun broke through the cirrus in the west, and silver light flew down through a swale of aspens on the far side of the reservoir. The thin clouds gave a ceiling that held color —a yellow-orange against the deeper blue. The same orange reflected in the water, but it was paler, mixed with the stir of the moving air over the surface. Wade held up his hand to shield his eyes from the angled light.

Terry was still following the basketball along the shore. He stepped over rocks and around a rotted wooden rowboat filled with sand. The breeze was carrying the ball toward a narrow spit that jutted out into the lake.

Wade made himself another gin and tonic, stronger than the first, and checked the far shore with his binoculars. Some of the women were building fires on the sand, and smoke rose and curled into the low light. One man reeled in an empty line and put away his tackle. Another put on more bait and cast angrily out toward Wade. Wade hadn't thought ever, before that moment, that he would die in Idaho. His notion of death—his own, anyway—was going to the hospital in Galveston and passing away in his sleep.

He scanned right. A car raised dust on the hill and turned into the trailer park and stopped. Wade made out some Indians in the front seat. One boy got out and let a girl out from the middle. She ran up the steps of a nearby trailer. The boy got back in, and the car spun its tires and turned down toward the ragged grove of cottonwoods along the creek.

Wade lowered the glasses and took a sip of his gin. "Don't go too far," he called to Terry. "We're going to eat pretty soon."

Terry didn't look around. He sat on the shore and took off his sneakers and socks and rolled up his pants' legs, and then he waded out toward the basketball.

Terry was a funny kid. What was in store for a boy whose only talent was dribbling a basketball? He was intense, quiet, smarter than his grades. When he was little, he loved bones of animals and birds he found on the beaches. He chiseled off the meat and skin, let the ants polish up, then bleached the bones in the sun. Wade thought this obsession was not normal.

"What's normal?" Dana asked. "He likes them."

"But don't you think it's odd?"

"Maybe he wants to know what's inside of things. If you're worried, why don't you ask him about it?"

Wade hadn't asked, and Terry had got over the fascination with bones. For a while he collected shells. Then it was stamps, coins, bottle caps. Wade got him a basketball when Terry was nine.

The breeze shifted, or there was a current around the spit, and the ball moved out farther into deep water. Terry, in water to his knees, backtracked to shore. The ball floated toward the center of the reservoir and then was carried northward. In the binoculars it looked to Wade like an orange sun on the burnished water. Behind it were riffles of gray and yellow, some insects hovering, glassy blue swells that seemed almost magical. A tern, nearly white, circled the ball once and then wheeled away.

He knew Terry wasn't coming back. The basketball was more important than dinner, and Wade's teasing hadn't helped. Discipline was impossible now that he saw Terry only sporadically. Events didn't occur on a daily basis, so there was no enforcement. Wade wanted to be liked, so Terry knew he could get away with anything. That was how things worked when history was broken.

Wade finished the gin and tonic and got out hamburgers, noodles, canned corn. What he really wanted to do was to take down the tent and stow the gear and go buy another basketball in Pocatello, but he couldn't disappoint Terry, so he fired up the campstove and put water on to boil and made himself another gin and tonic.

Wade wished he could get Terry to shoot. He could dribble like a fiend, but in Wade's mind he wasn't a player unless he could shoot. When Terry was twelve, Wade had taken him to tryouts for an age-group rec-league team, and Terry had been one of the first cuts. He was the best dribbler and could play man-to-man, but he couldn't make a layup or a free throw. Terry had taken it better than he had. If they wanted a shooter, too bad.

The basketball was out in the middle of the reservoir now, farther away than ever, and Terry ran barefoot along the shore. There was an inlet Terry had to skirt, and once Wade lost sight of him behind a hill. He took his gin and tonic to the far side of the knoll where he had a better view of the reservoir.

There were several fires now on the far shore, brighter now that the light had faded. One of the Indians shouted something and began to dance at the edge of the water, and Wade focused the binoculars on him. He'd had a strike—his fishing rod was bent and vibrating in his hands—and he scuttled along the shore, lifted his rod over another man's, laughed and whooped. One of the children drank from his beer can left behind, but most of them followed the fisherman, who kept reeling in. Several women shouted to him, and he answered something back that Wade couldn't understand.

It was a big fish. Wade saw it thrash in the water, and an old man brought over a net and waded out in rubber boots. He held the net poised, and the man with the rod tried to steer the fish toward him. But the fish swerved away and then jumped once and ran for deep water. The line broke.

Everyone on the shore looked after it for a moment, stunned. The water was placid, trackless. Then one of the women pointed to the basketball.

The ball was closer to the other side now, toward the shallow end where the creek flowed in. Wade couldn't tell how deep the creek was. There was a willow thicket there, and then cottonwoods beyond, and Terry was standing at the edge of the creek as if gauging whether he could cross.

"Come back," Wade shouted. He heard his own voice echo from the far shore.

But Terry, standing near the moving water, couldn't hear him. He stepped into the current and maneuvered his way from rock to rock and came out in the willows on the other side. Wade trained his binoculars on him. Terry worked his way through the brush and back toward the exposed mud-flats. It was dusk now, and the hills were gray. The sky ebbed to dark blue, though the last light was almost white in the west.

Just then the car with the Indian boys came out of the cottonwoods at the edge of the trailer court. Terry couldn't see them for the willows. The windows of the car were open, and the driver had his elbow out. The boy on the passenger side was smoking a cigarette and pointed out at the lake toward the basketball.

"Terry!"

Terry kept walking.

The car eased forward along the mudflat. A crowd had gathered now on the other side near the basketball—the fishermen, the women, the children. The car had stopped near the crowd of Indians, and the boys got out. The basketball floated nearer to the far shore. Terry came out from the brush and onto the flat, looked around, and kept walking. He wasn't afraid. It was his basketball.

Wade threw down his gin and tonic and called again, but he was too far away. He pulled the binoculars from around his neck.

"Terry!"

He unbuttoned two buttons of his shirt and started running, pulling at the buttons as he raced down the knoll. The Indians across the lake looked over. Terry stopped. Wade kept yelling.

"Terry!"

He careened down the slope and, at the bottom, shed his boots and pants. He ran toward the spit, still yelling wildly and waving his arms, and splashed into the shallows. He stepped as high as he could to keep speed, then suddenly fell forward into the cold water. He swam. The icy water made no difference. The gin gave him energy. He swam as fast as he could, but he tired quickly. The smooth gray swells moved away from him toward the light in the west, toward the green aspens and the fires, toward the orange basketball floating eye level in front of the Indians watching him, and toward his son on the dark shore.

EVERY DAY A PROMISE

MCCALLUM COULDN'T DESCRIBE THE FEELING. IF HE TRIED TO tell anyone, analogy was all he could use. It was like a blind spot in his vision, or trying to catch a fish that wasn't there, or losing something through a hole in his pocket. He never thought about it when he was younger because the feeling never existed. He never thought about things then, never considered the future. But the feeling existed now.

As a boy growing up in Hamden, Connecticut, he ran the narrow, tree-shrouded country roads after school not because he was in training, but because he wanted to. Even then, he had his sights set on records, though he didn't know what kind. His chest was thin and his body was all knees and elbows, but his legs had a piano-wire resilience, that spring.

Then he discovered his talent: high jumping. He set school-boy records in Connecticut, school and Ivy League records at Brown. He knew his ability. So when had the suspicion begun? He couldn't point to any particular hour or day or week.

The local bus on which McCallum was riding stopped, and he climbed down to the pavement. There was no one around—just the barren trees, the dark black brook at the bottom of the hill, a cold blue sky. He started up the hill, looking after the bus, whose tail of exhaust swirled in the cold air. He knew Hillary would be watching for the bus, would see it crest the hill ahead of him. She would start down the lane from her house to meet him. Why should he think this an imposition? He should have been pleased she was eager to see him.

Two years before, he had faced the best competition in the country at the National Meet in Atlanta. He had confidence then. He was able to put his mind outside the moment, outside himself. He measured his own height against that of the thin black-and-white bar set several inches above his head. From a standing position, he kicked his leg up, testing the height, envisioning his approach as if on a film clip. Then he loped to the back of the runway apron, tracing the steps of his approach. He moved deliberately, taking his time, breathing slowly and with precision. He turned defiantly and confronted the bar.

Number 14, New York Track Club. The bar was spun like a thread between the standards. Everything else disappeared; he did not see anyone else, or hear the crowd, or feel the slight back breeze. He stepped forward in an easy, loping stride, took a stutter step near the bar to gain the extra thrust he needed, and pushed off his left foot. He knew the lift, the movement of his body through the air, the exact instant, like a magician's sleight of hand, he had to kick the trailing leg. He knew everything there was to know at that moment, and he jumped a height he only rarely dreamed about.

Just over the crest of the hill, the lane to Hillary's house turned left and descended. It was shaded by maple trees, and on either side were vine-covered sheds and garages, so from the mouth of the alley he saw only green down the slope. Hillary came up the lane. She had on a pale blue shirt and her hair was pulled back. She waved from a quarter-mile away, and he was forced by her greeting to wave back.

He told himself: if you feel that way about her, tell her.

But he did not feel that way, really. He could not blame

her for his uncertainty. In fact, he admired her. She coped as a single mother, worked three days as a buyer for a clothing store and at home as a freelance editor the rest of the time. She maintained her house and her possessions. She had no bitterness. Her eyes that should have been hard were gentle; her smile that might have turned cruel from her experience had not. The past had not seemed to affect her much. McCallum wondered about that: no fuss, no emotion.

McCallum walked wearily down the lane. He was twenty-seven years old and worked in Warwick, Rhode Island, as a hospital aide. Nothing glamorous, but he was testing himself to see whether he wanted to apply to medical school. Did he have the temperament? The desire? He hadn't decided yet.

From the tangle of underbrush, the children suddenly sprang out, laughing. "Uncle Mac, Uncle Mac!" they shouted.

He threw up his hands in surrender, and the children laughed. John seven, and Marnie five, closed in on either side of him.

"Come with us," John said.

Each of the children pointed a stick gun at him.

"I'll do whatever you say," McCallum said.

They each grabbed hold of one of McCallum's arms and led him down the lane toward their mother. In their darkly tanned faces he saw traces of Hillary blended with another man he had never seen. Their eyes were round like Hillary's, their skin fair. The tan they got from being at the neighbor's pool was fading now they were back in school. They both had blond hair, though Hillary's was darkish red.

"We caught him," Marnie shouted.

"We want Uncle Mac to come with us to the park," John said. "Can he?"

What he'd thought was a pale blue shirt was a sweater. He had himself not thought of the chill and had on only a thin jacket. Hillary's hair was in a twist at the top of her head. She embraced him, kissed his cheek, steadied herself against him.

"What's at the park?" McCallum asked.

"We want you to see what we found," Marnie said.

"What is it?"

"You have to *see*," John said.

Marnie tugged at his arm. "It's not that far."

"Something dead," John said, as if dead things were more exciting than things alive.

"Uncle Mac has been at work," Hillary said. "He wants to rest."

Marnie stopped pulling his arm. "You don't want to come, Uncle Mac?"

"If it's dead it won't move," he said. "I'll come see it in the morning."

"Somebody might steal it," John said.

"You children go over to the Harrises' for a while," Hillary said. "Penny will be glad to play with you."

"I don't want to play with *her*," John said.

The children moved off slowly, looking back at McCallum as if he had betrayed them.

"Tomorrow," McCallum said.

Marnie whispered to John, and they broke into a run back up the lane toward the house.

"I've come to a conclusion," McCallum said. He and Hillary were sitting on the comfortable sofa in her sunroom, though it was night now, and the children were in bed.

"Decisions are good," she said.

He didn't look at her. "Well, that is, I've decided something, and I haven't."

"Which is it?"

He felt her watching him, sensed her effort not to be too eager to guess what he meant. The clock chimed. It was an antique, a medium-sized wall clock with a pendulum, placed next to the mantel. The mantel was littered with artifacts—glass birds, two silver candlesticks, and a goblet. There was a painting of irises on the wall opposite the clock.

"Where did you get all these things?" he asked.

"You're not going to tell me what you decided, or didn't decide?"

He leaned forward to the coffee table, where art books were piled up beside a Japanese vase and a carved ivory llama. "Like this thing," he said. He picked up the carved animal. "Did someone give it to you?"

"I bought it."

"Where?"

"In Buenos Aires."

"I know Buenos Aires," he said. "I was there for the Pan American Games. Were you there with your husband?"

"What have you decided, Mac?"

"How much was it?" he asked.

"I forget. I bought it from a street peddler."

"So it's not valuable?"

"It is to me. I keep it for luck."

He put the carving back on the table. "I've decided it's tomorrow or never," he said.

"What's tomorrow or never?"

"Something or nothing."

"You're being vague deliberately," Hillary said. "Why won't you say what you mean?"

"I won't compete if I don't think I can get better," he said. "It's not enough to meet expenses."

"But you love what you do."

"I've set a goal for tomorrow's meet," he said. "If I don't

make it, I'm through."

Hillary touched his arm gently. "I don't want you to do this for me," she said.

"I'm not doing it for you. I wouldn't do that."

"Sometimes I think you imagine what I want."

"I try not to imagine."

"I want you to do what you believe in."

And what was that? What did he believe in? He believed in *doing*, not in thinking. He wanted to grow up and stop believing he could jump heights he couldn't and had no hope for. There were younger jumpers with catapults in their legs, with new styles. He couldn't keep up with them forever.

And what *did* she want? They weren't married. Did she want to be? She would never have said it, or its complement: quit, Mac, before it's too late. "I'm doing it for myself," he said.

"Good," she said. "That's all I want."

He nodded and pulled his arm from hers and stood up. "I've got to get some sleep," he said.

He had rented the cellar apartment in Warwick more than a year ago, at the same time he'd taken a leave from M. F. Guadagno, the investment firm, to make a last try for the Olympics. He'd sold his car, borrowed from his mother. He wasn't sponsored—the younger jumpers had coaches and affiliations. He trained alone at a high school field for two months, running laps, sprints, the grandstand. He cross-trained playing racquetball. He refined his rituals for jumping: the order in which he removed his warm-ups, the steps, the exercises for breathing. Then just before the Trials, he'd pulled a hamstring doing hurdles and couldn't jump.

All he could do was rest. M. F. Guadagno took him back. His life resumed its former shape, but not his spirit. Failure moved him. After six months, he quit the investment business for good and got a part-time hospital job. He swam at the Y, resumed running slowly, strengthening his legs with distance.

Then one day as he ran hills, he turned down a road he had never been on before. At a blind corner a little boy on a bicycle nearly hit him. McCallum fell and scraped his arm; the boy slid sideways and crashed into high grass at the side of the road. A woman saw the accident and came running.

John was more hurt than he was—a sprained wrist—but he was brave and cried only as long as he was scared. McCallum carried the bike to the house, while John and Hillary walked. "Are you a marathon man?" the child asked.

"No, I'm a high jumper."

"But you're running."

"I'm training," McCallum said. "More or less."

"You're just talking now."

"You're right. Talking isn't training."

Hillary had mentioned her divorce right away. She never hid anything from him. What could she have hidden? It was public record. She won custody and support, no alimony. She didn't want his money.

A month later, she invited McCallum to live with her. It was very fast, but they had desperation in common. She felt freer with him there, and cared for at the same time. He liked the house, the children, the countryside of green trees and lanes, the far ridge visible from the back deck, the creek. The children called him Uncle Mac.

McCallum Pillsbury, reduced to Uncle Mac.

He liked the children, helped them with their homework, watched them while she was in New York or Boston on day trips buying clothes. But for McCallum, if his malaise had started anywhere, it had started with the children.

"Can we watch you jump, Uncle Mac?" John asked.

"You've seen me jump."

"In a meet, I mean. Where it counts."

"Sure."

"When?" Marnie asked.

"The next one."

"Promise?"

"I promise."

But he had not taken them with him to Indianapolis. Or to Dallas. Or even to Philadelphia, where he drove Hillary's car.

Promise. What else had he promised them? Every day was a promise: fixing them dinner when their mother was late, reading to them at night before bed, asking them about their friends at school. And every day was a lie.

The nights with Hillary were easy. He liked the hours after the children were in bed, the quiet space, the feeling, after so many years in bare rooms, that he was *somewhere else*. And in her bed they lay in the silence, holding each other, the moonlight sifting through the deep trees to her window. He touched her and heard her sigh from a great distance, felt himself sink into her sighs, as though he were disappearing and she were calling him to stay. He caressed her and held her tighter, and he knew all he had to do the rest of his life was to say yes.

He had not given up his cellar apartment. He hadn't meant to keep it, really. At first he had kept it as a place to dress when he worked out at the school nearby, a place to shower, a locker. The rent was so cheap. And it was near the hospital. After work he sometimes dropped by to water the geraniums he kept in the window, the narcissus. Then it became a place to be alone. That was when it became dangerous, when it became a secret.

"Where did you go after work?" Hillary asked him once.

"What do you mean?"

"I thought you got off at noon."

"I went to work out," he said.

"And after that?"

"I stopped for a beer at Chauncey's Bar. Did you need me for something?"

"No, I just wondered."

When he lied about it, the apartment became a necessity.

That was where he went that morning several hours before the meet in New York. He told Hillary he needed several hours alone to concentrate before the competition: it was part of his ritual.

The room was quiet, and he lay on the bed and stretched his body diagonally across the covers. He breathed deeply. Over the months he lived with Hillary he trained as hard as ever. No one could have been more disciplined. He did leg presses, Nautilus, isometrics, rode the bicycle. He jumped low heights with weights sewn in specially made shoes. He ate correctly and precisely, took supplements of vitamins and minerals, went to bed early. But sleep was another matter.

Now he felt what he had done was absurd—all the measuring of steps, the fiddling with takeoff angles and kicks and timing, the breathing and calisthenics. What did it matter? What did it mean to jump high?

He stopped stretching and lay on the bed, quietly. A low light came through the cellar window, through the green leaves of the unblooming geranium. What had John and Marnie wanted to show him? What dead thing? He imagined a squirrel poisoned, a pigeon killed by disease, a dog run over by a car. And why had he not gone to see it that morning as he promised? Instead he explained his ritual to Hillary —why he had to be alone before the meet. Before he left the house, before the children woke, he put the carved llama into his duffel bag.

The chill of the cellar room worked into him. How could he feel so lonely when he had Hillary's house to go to, when love was everywhere in the people who lived there? His muscles cooled, and he stretched again briefly. Then finally he got up and packed his sweat clothes into his duffel.

He came down the long tunnel from the dressing room and saw the infield filled with color and movement. After twelve years of competition he should have expected the jitters, the healthy nervousness, but he was surprised by what he felt now: not the notched-up energy he fought by concentrating on himself, but rather an unusual awareness of everything around him. The blues, oranges, and reds of the athletes' suits against the green backdrop of the infield, the sun's warmth and light, the slight breeze on his skin, other athletes jogging and stretching, the notion that what he was doing was not right.

He stopped at the mouth of the tunnel and looked across the crowd that filled the arena. Hillary wanted to bring the children later, but he said no, please don't. He listened to her voice in his head saying, "But you promised." And his saying, "They can't come."

He jogged down the ramp and across the infield to the high-jump area, waving to some of his friends taking calisthenics. Some of the events had already been run. The loudspeaker carried the first call for the 800 meters.

As he wandered across the high-jump apron, the edge came back to him. This was familiar ground, the place he knew. He set his mind on the task, closed out the voices around him, the movement, the colors and sunlight. He moved onto the grass, set down his duffel bag, and did stretches of his own design: knee bends throwing a leg to the side, back bends, scissor kicks. He knew what worked for him.

The others, all younger—faces he knew—had already done their warm-ups and measured their approaches on the composite apron. McCallum lay back and closed his eyes, lifted his legs, spread them wide, brought them together again. Hillary of course could have brought the children anyway. In the kaleidoscope of the crowd he'd never see them. He supposed, too, she could have discovered he'd taken the carved llama from her coffee table. If he had asked her whether he might take it for luck, she'd have said yes, of course. Take it. But he hadn't wanted to ask. He'd wanted to steal.

He did push-ups—ten, fifteen, twenty—touching his nose to the grass. His blue warm-ups absorbed the sun, and he felt a short sweat. Up on his feet, he did jumping jacks, though he had the sensation, spreading his arms and legs in rhythm, that he was breaking apart, arms and legs whirling through the air.

The younger jumpers shed their warm-ups, but McCallum waited for the event to be called, the competitors introduced. He stayed apart from the others, checked and rechecked his steps. He felt loose, as strong as he had ever felt. But he knew he was in his own world, the fate of everyone who tried to realize dreams.

He made a few practice jumps, then sat on the grass and took the llama out of his duffel. He had told Hillary he'd set a height he wanted to achieve, but he had set no height. He did not know what to expect of himself anymore. Seven-three? Seven-ten? Forty years ago no one had ever jumped seven feet, but now the world record was over eight. How did the human body evolve? Or was it the mind? What was good enough, when he spent his whole life believing in himself?

He passed on the first three heights below seven feet. He stretched anxiously while the other jumpers took their routine jumps. He kept warm by jogging. At the fourth height, when his name was called, he stripped off his sweatpants. Once again he walked forward and measured his stride to the bar. He gauged his own height to the bar set a foot above him. In his calm ritual, he walked back again, counting silently.

Facing away from the bar, he took a deep breath, then turned quickly and, without thinking at all, ran toward the bar. His stride was light, slow, speeding up to build momentum. He did a stutter step, planted his left foot, and shot up into the air. His right foot cleared, he turned his body over the bar and kicked his trailing left leg. Simple. He rolled and was over and fell into the spongy pit.

Easy, smooth. It was going to be a good day. He knew it and passed at seven-three. He sat on the grass and warmed himself in the sun. He cleared seven-five and seven-seven, and each time returned and sat beside the llama on the grass. The bar was raised again. Everything was possible. He was unthinking when his name was called. He stood up and stretched, did his ritual before the bar, then soared up and over.

He took a late-afternoon train out of the city, then the bus from the station. Hillary might guess when he would be home, so to make sure she or the children wouldn't see him, he got off two stops in front of the lane. The sun ebbed through the clear dusk and disappeared beyond the feathery hills, and the neighborhood sifted to darkness before his eyes. Leaves fell; he heard them skitter on the pavement. It was cold. He walked slowly, carrying his duffel over his shoulder, the carving in his bare hand.

He had set no record that afternoon, but he won. He outjumped the younger men. And he felt perfect. In the instant he went over the bar on his last jump, he felt resurrected, as if he had proved to himself again he was still alive. But it was a resurrection without joy. How could he have known he would feel bitter about winning, that triumph would be tainted by loneliness?

This gap in his spirit left him helpless: neither alive with anticipation, nor dead from the exhaustion of the years of physical effort. He felt the stress of not knowing what to do next.

He reached the lane and looked down the shrouded avenue. No one was there. John and Marnie were inside now, after dark. Hillary was not at the bottom of the hill watching for him. It was too cold out.

He turned and walked toward the house. He wanted to be certain, but there was no certainty. The pressing clarity of his vision did not permit certainty, though it demanded an answer. The closer he came to the house, the more he was repelled by it. And what would he say to Hillary when he told her he had won?

He slipped into the house through the sliding door onto the porch and walked across the rug to the den. He put the carving of the llama back on the coffee table, then went into the dining room. The wooden floor creaked under his weight.

"Who is it?" Hillary called.

"It's me," McCallum said.

Hillary came through the swinging door from the kitchen, trailing the sound of the television. "You frightened me." She gave him a kiss on the cheek and looked at him. "How did it go? We missed the sports news."

"The door was open," he said, turning back toward the den.

The children raced in through the swinging door. "Hi, Uncle Mac, did you win?"

"I won," he said.

"How high did you go?" Marnie asked.

"Higher than I am. Way up here." He held his hand above his head.

"Can we see you in the next one?" John asked.

"Are you the champion?" Marnie asked.

"The best," he said.

Hillary moved away and let the children closer.

"We went to the park," John said. "The dead thing is still there."

"No one stole it?"

"Will you come with us tomorrow?" Marnie asked. "We want to show it to you."

"Yes," he said. "Tomorrow. Tomorrow is Sunday, isn't it?"

He looked from John to Marnie and then to Hillary, who stood near the doorway not looking at him.

INSTANTS

IN WINTER THE FLAT PLAIN BEFORE THE MOUNTAINS IS A WHITE cover of blowing snow. On the plowed road, the snow swirls like dust. The stark white of the snowdrifts passes quickly out my side window. Today is cold sun.

A silver Toyota station wagon passes going about eighty on the straightaway. Three pairs of skis stripe the roof, undersides blue, yellow, orange. Denver license. The man in the backseat takes a long look at Carrie beside me. She smiles not at him, but at me.

I concentrate on the snow blown up by the passing car. The hard flakes curl, then rest. I imagine photographing the patterns as I once photographed sand dunes in wind, and I think of stopping. My equipment is in the back of the Jeep, but before I slow down, new gusts have changed everything.

At Colona, we ease down to forty on ice. Another hour at least to skiing. We pass slowly the dozen or so buildings of the town. The Toyota has stopped at the Sinclair for gas. Two young men in colorful sweaters stand by the pump, while the woman with them goes inside.

"Do you think they're going to Telluride?" Carrie asks.

"Don't know," I say. Her unnecessary question breaks the silence we've been riding in. "They could be going to Utah. How should I know?"

Carrie looks at me. Dark eyes. I do not mean to be short

with her. I mean something else I cannot tell her.

We cross a bridge over a river, pass the state park. It's clear today and the mountains in the distance are snow filled and sunlit. Clean.

At Ridgway, we turn right onto Highway 62. Carrie wants to stop for coffee, but we were late getting away from Colorado Springs. I think, yes, we'll stop, but the town disappears behind us. We're on the hill outside of town, then over it, and into the ranch country. The houses look bound up in snow for the winter. I wonder how the people survive.

On the upslope, the Toyota appears again in the rearview mirror. Its black bumper rushes at us. Again it overtakes us, turning up snow. The man in the back looks Carrie over once again and waves. She waves back. I try to gauge her expression, but she looks the other way.

"He likes you," I say.

She smiles, taking it as a compliment. The smile broadens her face. She looks pretty with her hair pulled back. Her eyes seem pleased.

"Should I pull up to them?"

Her smile continues. "No. Why would you?"

I press my foot on the accelerator. The old Jeep picks up speed slowly. I leave my foot down.

"Please," Carrie says.

But I keep the accelerator down. We are suspended in the moving car like drops of water at the tips of icicles, not knowing whether we will freeze or fall.

I slow for a right turn, hug the hill. The Jeep is too high-clearance, and it slides. I let up on the gas and pump the brakes. A burst of sun hits from behind the hill.

The recognition of something on the road strikes me before it does Carrie. I press hard on the brakes: Carrie jerks forward, but grabs the dash in time. I hold the wheel.

Space evaporates between us and the unmoving shattered cars on the road.

To the left of the wreck is room enough to squeeze through. The silver Toyota lies crushed against a yellow Cadillac. Steam rises from the two engines into the cold air. The Toyota's horn is stuck, and its tone changes as we inch by. Steel mashed and slanted skyward, hood crushed. Skis ripped apart, glass shattered.

Someone in the Cadillac stirs, but in the Toyota no one moves. The driver's head is wedged between the door and the body of the car; the woman lies over the hood. Carrie's friend in the backseat sits with his head bent forward.

An instant.

I lift my sun goggles up onto my knitted cap. From the top of the mountain at Telluride, the earth spreads out like a white apron covering a lap. Pockets of houses below are folded into the creases. Over the valley, the skyline is only and all mountains.

I believe I'm not mortal. The morning's accident is in the past. I am a bird who can fly the length and the breadth, and in the anticipation of my flight, I know no bounds. Convictions, not thoughts, are in my mind. Born: the certainty that lives are hollow when two people are no longer of use to one another. I am thinking of Carrie.

I pull the goggles into place again and the sky turns yellow-blue. The straps of my ski poles fit tightly around the backs of my wrists. With leg and pole together, I push away from my perch.

Impetus delivered, I glide. To my right the mountain drops off precipitously to the basin below. I dig the edge of the ski inward and lean outward over the hill. Snow hisses beneath me. Whatever I need I have learned long ago and do

not think about. Weight farther back in the powder, tuck and
lift up. It is not like other things.

I stop again. Far down in the valley, Carrie skis easier terrain. She is foolishly afraid to ski here with me, and I am
foolishly afraid to ski there with her. Where I stand now, the
mountain cuts off the wind. In the quiet I pick out a cloud
and watch it move across the mountains. Clouds are scarce
today. The cloud reminds me how lazy I am. I cannot muster
my strength to hold on to people. It would seem that such a
lazy person would content himself to hold on to one.

Without thinking, the weight moves. I barely make con-
tact with the snow. Pole and spring up. I angle cross-country
toward the manicured trail. I hurry, as though I have seen
something to fear. I make a run for it.

Full speed, I hit a drop-off. In the air my body sinks quickly,
though my mind waits. I lurch and lose balance. My poles
flip out underneath, and one ski drags. Its tip catches, and I
jerk forward, arms outstretched. The first puff of snow hits
my goggles. The binding snaps open.

On the second impact—the bounce—the pain stings my
knee.

I have been drinking Scotches for an hour and have limped
back and forth to the bathroom. Carrie has gone to the room
to rest, and I wait for her. A stranger notices my cast. "Today?"
he asks, pointing. He has on a gray sweater, lighter than his
hair, baggy pants, and slippers. The pouches under his eyes
make him look weary.

I nod, and he smiles. "Broken?"

His questions in one word bother me for no reason. "Torn
ligaments," I say.

"Could have been worse, huh?"

"Could have been dead." I think of the accident that

morning. The lightness of my tone frightens me.

He begins a life story, how he got where he got.

Carrie comes in, sleepy-eyed from a nap. The man looks her over as she crosses the room.

"Profession?" he asks me.

"Freelance photography. Travel, fashion, on-the-scene assignments. Almost whatever I can get."

"I don't like the press," he says. He goes on thinking aloud that the press has sponsored the terrorism and the divisions in this country. I sip my Scotch as he starts to rave.

Carrie takes my arm, as though she knows what's coming into my head. I listen to the man, and the room wavers like heat over a radiator.

"Come on," Carrie says, "let's go."

I stand up, but continue to listen, and listen until I'm not hearing words, but only the voice. The puffy skin under the man's eyes gets me.

"Please," Carrie says.

The man calls the press liars and opportunists of the worst sort.

"Hey!" I shout.

He looks at me and stops talking. For the first time he sees me. I can tell by his eyes. My fist rushes forward from my chest and connects to the right of his nose and a little above the mouth. I miss the sacks under his eyes.

I reach down and take Carrie's hand away.

"I've been drinking too much," I tell her. My voice comes disembodied from the air. I open my eyes and expect to see the voice, but there's only the darkness of the room.

Carrie puts her head on my chest and rests her hands there, too. Her warmth is so genuine I can't disbelieve it.

"What are you thinking?" she asks.

"Nothing."

I wonder in the silence whether anyone can think nothing.

Carrie moves. "Sometimes you shut me out so tightly," she says.

She sits up on the bed in the dark. Her nakedness moving away is our nakedness together.

She does not cry.

We met three months before in Colorado Springs on one of my assignments to photograph an exhibit she'd arranged at the fine-arts center. I see her there as though in a photograph—brilliant dark hair, dark eyes, yellow dress. Though now the light has gone.

Lying on a picnic blanket one night in the foothills, she at first said no. She was the one with too much to lose. Then in the dusk, the world dissolved around us, and timeless, she said yes. It no longer mattered what she lost. She couldn't help it. I remember still her short hair then, and her wide-lipped mouth, and later her hand shaking as she bent her cigarette over a match flame in the car.

The sheets rustle as she turns to me again. "There must be some other way for us to go on," she says. "When it's like this I don't know where I stand."

"I don't know where I stand, either."

"With me you know."

I cannot answer. I am running. I grasp at one thing and another, to hold on to anything for a moment to give me support, but nothing is solid. It's painful to have everything slip beyond my reach. But after a while, pain is no different from the absence of pain.

Finally I say, "With me you know, too."

We lie together a long time. We return to the familiar warmth. Sleep: I hear her breath, and at last edge away from touching her.

In the middle of the night I wake and turn to her. She does not resist, but eases toward me in the bed. Connection of the most superficial sort, almost like a glance.

That realization sends me running again, mindless, with the white snow rushing past me. My legs are running, and in the darkness the silence is broken by Carrie's breathlessness.

Then it happens. At last the running slows. I breath again, glad to come back.

Instants. My first memory of particles was one afternoon as a child when the sunshafts came into my room through the windows. The light illuminated millions of particles of dust floating in the air. I swept my hand through the shafts of light, stirring the particles. But always they returned to floating, in and out of the light, according to the currents of the air. One moment I could see them, and the next they had passed the border of light into shade and had disappeared.

Instants. The instant of a shutter. The sand dunes. The pattern of snow curls on the road. The film freezes the moving particles. Beyond the shutter, the particles in life continue to move. A bird in flight continues to soar.

I have often sat alone in my darkroom hanging these instants along a wire. I have divided life into moments, particles of time. At what point does a heart flutter in the womb? I have stood before a trayful of negatives for hours, wondering what I have done to myself.

It is sleep coming to me. A few minutes have passed since Carrie and I made love. I drift in the moment before sleep like the particles of dust through the sunshafts of my room, not knowing whether I am in the sunlight or in the shadow.

THE INVISIBLE

THE MAN CRANED HIS HEAD OVER THE SALADS IN THE GLASS display case—potato, macaroni, lettuce-cucumber—while Orchard was making his pastrami sandwich. She was aware of him—something odd. He was smallish, maybe in his early thirties, curly hair, blue eyes intense. She had noticed him a couple of days earlier, too.

"Shyness is a protective covering," the man said. "It inhibits self-discovery."

Orchard stopped chewing her Dentyne and looked up. "Are you talking to me?"

"It's a camouflage," the man said. "You don't permit yourself to escape self-images. That's a grave danger, very grave."

Orchard pushed the pastrami sandwich onto the top of the counter above the meats and salads. "Please stay back from the sneeze guard," she said. "Mustard and mayonnaise are by the water cooler."

The man leaned forward and touched the plate gently. "My name is Renner," he said. "Kurt Renner. I teach at the college. 'Teach' is not the precise term. Words are insufficient. But I urge you to think about what you might become."

Orchard chewed her gum harder and put her hand on her hip. "Yeah, like what?" she asked.

"I don't know exactly," Renner said. "But just looking at you, I sense a sharpness, an acuity of spirit, a healthy appetite."

"A good body, you mean."

"Tell me about your family," Renner said.

"I have two younger sisters and a mother. My dad is a jerk. He likes my hair long." Orchard paused. "Look, mister, people are behind you in line. You want something else?"

"A quarter pound of macaroni salad," he said.

She spooned it into a plastic dish, covered it with a lid, and slid it across the counter. "Next," she said.

Renner moved off toward the cash register.

Solomon Sloan was six-three, two hundred pounds. He could throw a football sixty yards in the air and twenty through a swinging tire. In his sophomore year he had broken the college records for pass completions and yardage in a single season, and in the first three games of his junior year, he'd almost single-handedly defeated two good football teams and annihilated a mediocre one. But he was flunking Basic Mediums of Communication.

"I mean, it's a gut, man," said Carlos Druce, the wideout. "Even I, Carlos the Dunce, am making a B."

"You're not stupid," Solomon said.

"Is the man going to ineligible you?"

"He has the snipers looking," Solomon said. "What a bastard. Just because he's written the book."

"He's making a fucking *mint*," Carlos said.

"So will we," said Solomon, "if we ever get out of school."

"I mean, all that unconscious stuff," Carlos went on. "The vibes, like. Have you not been in an elevator with a woman and wondered what you were saying to her just *standing* there?"

"I'm a literalist," Solomon said.

"I mean, like, by shifting your feet or gazing with your eyes?"

"Usually you gaze with your eyes," Solomon said. "If I

have something to say, I say it."

"You *intuit* what she wants," Carlos said, "and she *intuits* what you want."

"Carlos, you don't have to shift your feet. Every woman knows what you want."

"But how can you be getting an F? We have a *football team*. You are the passer, and I am the receiver. Go see the professor, man. If you don't pass, I don't catch the ball. If I don't catch the ball, I don't get a pro *contract*."

"Or the woman in the elevator," Solomon said.

The next afternoon Solomon waited nervously in Renner's reception area. The door to the office was open, and now and then Renner looked up from his word processor and fixed Solomon with a stare. Some students thought Renner was brilliant because he'd written six books, including the course text *Borders*, which Solomon thought should have been called *Boredoms*. Renner didn't call him inside, so Solomon waited.

He didn't know what he'd done to get an F for a midterm grade. There had been no papers, no quizzes, no exam. Renner lectured in a pedantic style and a singsong voice punctuated with long pauses that, Renner said, were opportunities to explore. Sometimes Renner showed weird foreign films in which almost nothing was said, even in subtitles. Sometimes he called students to the front of the classroom to demonstrate some theory or other that, Solomon admitted, he never understood. In fact, Renner called Solomon up once and made him stand with his back to the class, as if that showed something more than a rear end and broad shoulders.

As he waited, Solomon felt Renner's disgust for him work through the pores of his skin. Probably Renner hated him because he played football. That was all Solomon could come up with. It was the natural jealousy of the small for the strong, of the clumsy for the coordinated, of the bumbler for the gifted athlete. And yet in this confrontation, Renner clearly had the upper hand. Solomon checked his watch and whispered under his breath, "Come on, you dry turd, come on. I'll be late for practice."

After forty-five interminable minutes, Renner glanced up and nodded for Solomon to enter. Solomon was furious.

Renner stood up from his word processor as soon as Solomon came into the room. He moved to a small lectern near his desk. There was a noticeable difference between the reception area and the inner sanctum. The interior office was smaller and had tension in it, a palpable heat, and the air was so tight Solomon couldn't speak.

"I know why you've come," Renner said calmly.

The room eased slightly.

"Coach Blake sent me."

"It's a common ailment," Renner said. He studied Solomon carefully.

"What is?"

Renner smiled briefly. There was a long pause. The room compressed again. "All right, Mr. Sloan, I won't make you ineligible. But on one condition."

"Name it," Solomon said.

"You must transfer into my seminar."

"But that's a four-hundred level," Solomon said. "I'm failing the beginning class."

"That's the deal," Renner said. "If you attend every week, I guarantee you an A."

"You mean just show up."

"You have great potential, Mr. Sloan. Is that so much to ask?"

*　*　*

Orchard Miller had grown up not far from the college in Willingham Heights, a neighborhood of third- and fourth-generation houses between the city and the suburbs. Her father was an upholsterer, and her mother taught third grade. Her two sisters, Dawn and Missy, had gone to the college, but Orchard hadn't.

"Why not?" Renner asked. "Why didn't you go on?"

"I wanted to get out of town," Orchard said.

"But here you are," Renner said, touching her arm. "You are not an illusion."

They were sitting in a booth in a Chinese restaurant, where Renner had ordered a mai-tai for her and a Tsingdao beer for himself.

"No, I'm not an illusion," Orchard said. "At least I don't think so."

She had sought out Renner the day after he ordered the pastrami sandwich in the deli. He was the first person who offered her real help. At least she thought he offered. The questions he posed churned through her mind all that afternoon and evening. Was she so shy? What could she become? She felt things were going by so fast she couldn't catch up.

Most men were kinder to her for her figure than for her ambition. The manager of the Food Bear, where she worked before, used to sidle into her checkout stand and rub against her—checking the cash register, he said. And the deli owner had at first told her there was no job. Then he'd called her the next day. "I want to try a new marketing technique," he said. "You. I like your body."

She let herself be used: that was her conclusion. She wasn't going to be used again.

When the drinks came, Orchard stuck her gum under the table and sipped her mai-tai.

"What else do you have your heart set on?" Renner asked.

"What do you mean, 'what else'?"

"Besides escape."

Orchard squirmed in her seat. "Well, at one time I wanted to be a singer. I used to sit on the roof of our house and sing to the moon."

"The moon is a cold audience," Renner said. He poured the Tsingdao into his glass and waited for the foam to ebb.

"I used to dream of running," Orchard said.

"What else?"

"I suppose once I wanted to fall in love."

"How old are you?" Renner asked.

"Nineteen."

"Do you see you can do all these things?"

"I have time, I guess," Orchard said, "if that's what you mean. But being young hasn't done anything for me yet."

"See beyond time."

Orchard did not see, but she felt a twinge of something in herself, something she couldn't put a word to. Renner didn't say anything, and she smiled nervously and glanced at the menu, which was written in Chinese.

"Let me order for you," Renner said.

The first meeting of the seminar was as strange as Solomon's interview. At every seat around the oval table were two ground rules printed on a card:

(1) YOU MUST SIT IN THE SAME SEAT AT THE TABLE EVERY WEEK.

(2) YOU MUST PAY ATTENTION.

Pay attention to what? Solomon wondered. Nothing happened. No one at the table opened a book to the reading assignment. Renner didn't speak. The class was silent.

For a while Solomon fended off boredom by concentrating on the A he would earn if he endured the tedium three hours a week. It wasn't a bad thought. But it was hard to think of grades for very long. He tried to focus on football, but was surprised he couldn't conjure up the big plays even from the previous week. And the other daydreams that were reliable in econ and sociology—usually about women—didn't materialize either.

After twenty minutes, Renner got up, picked up the stool he'd been sitting on, and made a place for himself a third of the way around the table. He sat down directly across from Solomon and didn't say anything. Solomon noticed the girl beside Renner—a brunette with short hair, and eyes of smoky quartz. He gazed at her, but had no luck. The girl closed her eyes as if she were going to sleep. On the other side of Renner was a creepy, frazzle-headed boy with glasses, and Solomon tried to intimidate him with a steady stare. The boy averted his eyes. It was the longest class Solomon had ever been to.

That Saturday was the first conference game. As usual, Coach Blake gave an inspiring speech in the locker room. They were the visitors. The crowd was hostile, but if they kept the ball, the crowd wouldn't be a factor. Silence the crowd, Coach Blake said. Eleven guys could make sixty thousand people shut up.

On the first three series of downs, Solomon was sluggish. He missed receivers, including a wide-open Dunce, and their punter had to kick three times. Then on the fourth series, Solomon fumbled on his own twenty-two-yard line, which set up an easy touchdown. Trying to compensate for the fumble, Solomon threw an interception that led to a field goal. It was 10-0 at the half, the crowd was thundering for blood, and Coach Blake was furious.

In the second half, though, Solomon came alive. His passes were precision darts to the soft spots in the opponents' zone coverage, and when the defense went man-to-man, Solomon checked off at the line of scrimmage and sent Carlos Druce deep on a fly pattern. When Carlos turned to look back for the ball, the rainbow fell right onto his fingertips.

Solomon threw scoring strikes on three consecutive possessions, and by the fourth quarter, when the reserves went in, Solomon was laughing and counting his cash on the sideline.

"Shyness is an attempt to make people guess who you are," Renner said. "Sing me a song."

Orchard looked over the deli counter. There were four people sitting at tables by the window. She was fixing potato salad. "I don't want to sing you a song."

"Why not? Are you protecting an image of yourself? What difference could it possibly make to these people here, even if they didn't want to hear you sing?"

"Why do you think they don't?"

"Precisely," Renner said. He smiled at a woman sitting at the window, then turned back to Orchard. "What kind of car do you drive?"

"Car?"

"How do you get to work?"

"I drive."

"So what kind of car?"

"A dented car."

"What model?"

"Volkswagen."

"Color?"

"Yellow. What kind of car should I drive?"

"It's not a question of should. What does the car tell about you? Or rather, what do you choose to tell people about yourself?"

"I like my car," Orchard said.

Renner smiled. "Suppose we try an experiment."

"I'm not going to sing," Orchard said. She sampled the potato salad.

"I want you to go to a football game with me this Saturday."

"What kind of football game?"

"How many kinds are there?" Renner asked.

At the next seminar something in the room was new. Solomon felt everyone looking at him as if he were guilty of a crime. They didn't stare at him exactly, but they cast surreptitious glances his way. He felt his fly must be undone, but it wasn't, and anyway, he was sitting down. His face burned; his lips dried up. The silence absorbed him like quicksand.

Renner must have said something to the others. That was all Solomon could think of to explain the phenomenon, though it was true his picture had been in the newspapers for leading the comeback victory over Tech. He'd completed twelve of fourteen passes in the second half and had kept the team undefeated. So why were the other students looking at him *that* way?

No one said anything, of course; that wasn't allowed. But he felt their eyes were microscopes to their minds. All the hostility the students could muster was aimed at him. And for no reason. He'd done well on the field. He'd led the team to victory.

After class he was so shaken he went to Renner's office. He was admitted right away.

"What can I do for you?" Renner asked. He was standing at the lectern.

"I want to transfer back to the regular class," Solomon said.

"You're failing the regular class. Besides, you've missed two weeks' work."

"I'll make it up."

Renner smiled. "You're afraid. Is that it?"

Solomon didn't answer.

"Why should you be afraid of a dozen students when you have thousands watching you on Saturday afternoons?"

"I don't know."

"You've improved," Renner said.

"Improved how?"

"Mr. Sloan, why do you insist on linear measurement? Why do numbers mean so much to you—yards, completions, *grades?* Why are they so crucial?"

"I want a pro contract."

"Ah, you have aspirations!"

"I think I do, yes."

"And you define yourself by these goals?"

"If I pass for enough yards, someone will knock on my door," Solomon said. "I'd be happier with five million than with one million."

"Do you define love by the number of women you've possessed?"

Solomon did not blink. "I don't see the connection."

"I presume you've heard of love."

"Vaguely. It's the opposite of hate."

Renner sighed. "Linear again."

"I felt hatred in there today."

Renner leaned over the lectern. "I have promised you something, Mr. Sloan. I mean to keep my promise. It's my obligation to help you. I can't let you go back to Basic Mediums when you've come this far."

"How far is that?" Solomon asked. "One to ten?"

Orchard didn't like football, and she had to work Saturday afternoon to fill the gas tank on her VW. "I've got to pay rent," she told Renner.

"I'll give you the equivalent of double overtime."

"To go to a football game?"

"What have I been to you but honest?" he asked. "There will be a crowd. If you're going to sing, you have to get used to people."

"I'm not going to sing in a football stadium."

"There's someone I want you to see."

"I thought I would sing at Kokomo Joe's," Orchard said. "They have an open-mike night. Who do you want me to see at a football game?"

"I'll pay you triple overtime," Renner said. "And pay your rent. All you have to do is watch the game."

In the dressing room, lockers banged open and closed, and familiar voices like war chants sounded the enthusiasm of game day. Solomon and Carlos Druce sat side by side on the trainers' benches, getting their ankles taped. The training room smelled of liniment spray, muscle rub, oranges, and Suregrip.

"So what's with the nerves?" Carlos said. "You throw 'em, and I'll snag 'em."

"I didn't sleep last night."

"Oh, yeah? Who was she?"

"It wasn't a she."

Carlos looked at Solomon carefully. The trainer taping Solomon's ankle looked up.

"It was an *it*," Solomon said.

Carlos smirked. "An it? Since when are you into animals?"

"Not animals," Solomon said. "Confusion, loss, and big-time malaise."

Carlos flexed his leg and set his other ankle down to be taped. "I thought malaise was what you put on a bacon-lettuce-and-tomato."

"I'm going to fail," Solomon said.

"Renner's giving you a fucking A, man. The guy guaran-fucking-teed it."

"I mean today," Solomon said. "On the field. Coach Blake shouldn't put me out there."

"Who *else* would he put out there?" Carlos said. "Who else can throw that stinger on the curl? Who else can throw the pig knuckles onto my sweet sensitive little tippy fingers?"

"That was last week."

"You got a different arm from last week? You got a new set of triceps? You got different feet, quads, hamstrings?"

"I've got a different brain," Solomon said.

"In one week?"

Orchard had never seen such a wild throng of people as spilled around outside the stadium that Saturday afternoon. A thousand vendors hawked programs and banners and sou-venirs. Renner bought her a purple-and-white pom-pom for the home team. "What do I do with this thing?" she asked, waving it in the air.

"You're a fan," Renner said. "You're supposed to express yourself."

She jabbed the stick end into Renner's ribs. "How's that?"

Even with the pushing and shoving to get into the stad-ium, Orchard was not prepared for what she saw at the end of the tunnel. So many colors overwhelmed her—the green field, the sunlit whites, the brilliant reds and blues in the crowd on the other side of the stadium. The home team's purple-and-white uniforms and gold helmets looked so crisp and clean she was overcome with joy. She had never heard so many people cheering.

"You won't tell me who you want me to see?"

"It's an experiment, remember?"

She followed Renner to their seats behind the home

team's bench.

Nothing much happened in the game that Orchard could see. After the kickoff, neither team mounted an offense. The opposition Bisons ran a few plays and kicked the ball, and so did the purple-and-white. Orchard wondered about the rules, but Renner didn't know much about football, either. He stared at the field and shrugged.

Once when the crowd groaned, Orchard asked the woman next to her what was going on. One group of home-team players moved slowly off the field while another group ran on. "Interception," the woman said.

"An interception is bad?"

"It is for our side," the woman said. "It's awful. We want completions. That's what Solomon is famous for." The woman pointed at a player near the bench who had taken off his helmet and stood dejectedly beside an angry man wearing earphones.

"Is that Solomon?" Orchard asked. "The one with the earphones?"

"The other one," the woman said. "He's the quarterback. Where have you been all your life?"

Orchard didn't know what a quarterback was, but she felt sorry for him. She stood up and waved her pom-pom, and yelled, "Go Solomon!" though her voice was drowned out by the cheering from across the stadium. Orchard sat down again and turned to Renner. "He's the one, isn't he?" she asked. "That boy who's so sad."

Solomon's failure was worse than he anticipated. The short passes he tried early—swing passes and buttonhooks —didn't connect, and when he wanted to get the running game in gear, the linebackers plugged the gaps. The crowd became impatient. A disappointed home crowd was worse than a hostile away crowd any day, and Solomon felt the pressure in the huddle. Instead of the confidence he usually had, he was shaky. He called a down-and-out to Carlos.

"Hit me, man," Carlos said. "This one is for the lady in the elevator."

Solomon barked signals, took the snap, faded back. He scanned the field for Carlos running his route. Solomon realized before he let go of the ball he was going to throw a terrible pass. But the arm was cocked, so he let it go. The ball wobbled through the air well short of the sprinting Druce, who had cut to the sideline. The safety in the short zone picked off the ball and waltzed down the field for a touchdown. The crowd booed. Solomon walked off the field.

"Jesus, Sloan, what was that?" Coach Blake yelled.

"It's the voids, Coach," Solomon said.

"The voids. Tell that to the pro scouts."

"Take me out."

"You just throw the goddamned football."

Solomon threw three more times—two incompletions and another pick. The team lost 17-3.

The day after the football game Orchard began running. She started from the stoop in front of her apartment building and jogged around the block. She thought she'd die. She rested ten minutes, then ran again. All she could think of as she gulped air was the quarterback sitting on the end of the bench with his head in his hands.

On open-mike night, she took her guitar to Kokomo Joe's and signed up on the performing list. Most of the singers were young and not very good, but Orchard admired their courage. She listened to a girl imitate Joni Mitchell, a college boy sing an off-key rendition of "What'll You Give Me if I Do?" and an old black man playing a blues harp. The longer she waited, the more troubled she became. All the performers had friends there who stomped their feet and clapped and gave high fives. She'd thought being anonymous would be a blessing. She thought she wouldn't be embarrassed. But instead she felt lonely.

When her name was called, she didn't answer or go forward to play. She sat and cried.

The next Saturday she went to the football game alone, and though she had general admission, she finagled her way to a seat behind the players' bench. Solomon started the game, and the first time his team had the ball, he was sacked and fumbled. The jeering was scattered at first, then died away gradually. Solomon, standing beside the man with the earphones, held his hands out, palms up, in supplication.

The purple-and-white held on downs, and after a punt, Solomon ran out onto the field again. He handed the ball to another player, who ran with it around the end. Then he handed off to a player behind him who was tackled right away. On third down, Solomon dropped back to pass. He threw over the middle, but the ball died in the air and fell harmlessly to earth.

"No! No! No!" The man with the earphones threw his clipboard to the ground.

The boos were louder. Orchard felt the crowd behind her was a huge wall of angry water held back only by a flimsy curtain.

"Go home, Sloan," someone shouted.

"Open up a new can of quarterbacks."

"He's been reading his press clippings," said a woman two rows back.

The jeers kept on, and at halftime Orchard called Renner from a pay phone under the stands.

"Is this the experiment?" she asked.

"What?"

"I can't go through with it," she said.

"Can't go through with what? Are you all right? Where are you?"

"I can't watch. He's awful. Worse than awful. Everyone boos."

"You mean Solomon Sloan?" Renner asked. "Are you at the game?"

"I want to comfort him," Orchard said.

Renner paused on the line. "Meet me—let's say Wednesday —in Woolworth's. Do you know where the photomat is?"

"Where you take your own picture?"

"Four-thirty," Renner said. "After my class."

Wednesday in the seminar Solomon was more depressed than he'd ever been in his life. Everyone knew about the game, of course. The highlights were on ESPN and on the TV news, and the sportswriters described the debacle in the newspapers. He fumbled once and threw four interceptions, and it was 28-0 before the coach pulled him. Solomon was still uncertain how it happened, what he did wrong, how he could go from so high to so low in a couple of weeks. The future he planned on—the big money, the Lexus, celebrity golf, the *house*—all of it—was hazy now, no more real than anyone else's dreams of glory.

He stared at the wooden tabletop.

"Concentrate," Renner said.

The word came from nowhere. Solomon had never heard Renner speak in the seminar before. He looked up. The pasty-faced curly-headed boy with glasses had pity in his eyes. Pity! The brunette with short hair smiled at him.

"What's this all about?" Solomon said.

"Mr. Sloan, there are *rules,*" Renner said.

The silence resumed. Interminable silence. Cursed silence. Blessed silence. Silence was lying; silence was telling the truth. The class scorned him and empathized; they hated him and loved him.

After class, Renner asked Solomon to come to his office.

Solomon resigned himself to demotion to Basic Mediums. He would be ineligible. The pro scouts would vanish. He would go back to being Solomon Sloan, whoever that was. He would graduate in six years, work in accounting, and live in New Jersey.

Solomon walked into Renner's reception area with a heavy heart. He'd have to wait, of course, maybe an hour, maybe two hours. He would have all those minutes to make things worse.

But Renner met him at the office door. "We're going out," he said. "I'm going to show you the invisible."

"What's that?" Solomon asked.

Renner led the way down the stairs. "Most people glimpse only reflections of themselves," Renner said. "They can't admit anything to the vital interior, nor, sadly, are they able to give anything from it. Are you following me?"

"At a distance," Solomon said.

They walked outside and across the quad.

"Do you believe every person you meet answers a personal question?"

"I've never considered it," Solomon said.

"Think of the seminar and what it means. Aren't the others mirrors that give back to you a picture of yourself?"

"Right."

"But the mirrors only give us images and, as we've learned, we are not images, are we?"

"I guess not."

"We are not statistics."

"I used to be statistics," Solomon said, "until the last two games."

"What we seek is our true selves, uncorrupted by images, unmeasured by numbers. We seek the invisible within us. That's what we've been trying to get at."

Solomon paused on the sidewalk. "We have?"

Renner jaywalked the street, and Solomon crossed after and caught up with him down the block near the Woolworth's. "But how do we know the invisible?" Solomon asked.

"We must either indulge or withdraw."

Solomon nodded. "Which have you done?" he asked.

"I teach," Renner said, "though not quite." He stopped at the entrance to the Woolworth's—a revolving door standing idle—and held out his hand, pointing the way. "You must see what's inside you."

"In Woolworth's?" Solomon asked.

"Let yourself go to any extreme."

Renner pushed Solomon into one of the wedges of the revolving door, and Solomon moved through. He came out by the photomat and looked around for Renner, who was not there.

Solomon Sloan delivered the football team four more brilliant Saturdays and a bowl bid. Orchard ran a 5K in 18:46 and the 10K Turkey Day Road Race in 38:05. Solomon made three As and one B. Orchard sang in Kokomo Joe's, and Solomon clapped and stomped his feet. Solomon turned down a pro football contract worth $5.4 million. Orchard went home to her family and took Solomon with her.

"Why, Orchard, you got your hair cut," her mother said.

"I've been discovering my true self," Orchard said. "I don't care whether Daddy likes my hair or not."

"I'll bet that's not all you've been doing," her father said, eyeing Solomon. "Who is this guy?"

"Solomon Sloan, sir." Solomon extended the hand that had thrown for 2,435 yards in a season.

Orchard's father ignored the hand. "You been helping my daughter with this discovery stuff?"

"I'm a quarterback," Solomon said.

"You're so thin, Orchard," her mother said.

"I've been running ten miles a day," Orchard said. "I've lost fifteen pounds."

There was a sudden long silence. Orchard's mother smiled the uncomfortable smile of fear for her daughter's safety. Her father sat down in his naugahyde chair in front of the TV. Orchard and Solomon exchanged glances across the room.

"So how did you two come together?" Orchard's mother asked.

"We met in Woolworth's," Solomon said.

"There was a man named Renner who used to come into the deli where I worked," Orchard said.

"He was my professor," said Solomon.

"Solomon and I took pictures of each other in the photomat," Orchard said. "I don't know how to explain it."

"Renner gave us a gift," Solomon said.

"A gift?" Orchard's father looked around. "What kind of gift?"

"He let us be who we are," Solomon said.

"Obviously some nut," said Orchard's father.

"He sounds wonderful," Orchard's mother said. "Maybe he could help your father."

Orchard crossed the room and held Solomon's hand. "The strange thing is, we don't know where he is. We went to show him the photographs we took, and his office was locked."

"He abandoned his classes," Solomon said. "He left his grades with the dean."

"It was as if he *knew* something," Orchard said, "and yet..."

"It's the invisible," Solomon said.

There was another long silence, and Orchard and Solomon gazed at one another, smiling.

PROJECTIONS

"We are not a nation of sheep, but a nation of forecasters."
—Darwin Hogan

1. (1961)

HARRIET SUTTON KNOCKED SO SOFTLY ON THE DOOR TO
the principal's office that when a voice responded, she edged
back and took a deep breath. Outside, beyond the windows,
children shouted on the playground, and Hank's voice rose
above the voices of the others. Harriet went in, and a pleasant-
looking young blond woman in a plaid dress greeted her.

Harriet clutched the doorknob. "I'm sorry my husband
couldn't come," she said. "He works, you know."

"It's all right, Mrs. Sutton. Please sit down. I'm Amy
Lowery."

"I work, too," Harriet said.

She sat down on the straight chair in front of the desk,
and Amy Lowery handed her a sheaf of papers. Harriet
gazed at the top page without seeing it.

"This report summarizes our recommendations," Amy
Lowery said. "As you can see, we've dated each of the inci-
dents and our observations of Hank's behavior, and the
teacher who made the report has initialed it. Some of these

events you've heard about before."

The words Harriet read made no sense to her. She felt a quickening of guilt, then anger, remembering she had always been the one to answer Hank's night-cry. She, not Judd, had always been the one to rock him, back and forth, back and forth, for hours.

"Our recommendations, of course, are not binding on you in any way. We report our impressions, but you and your husband must decide what's best for Hank."

Harriet nodded, but the woman's tone irked her. What was she saying? That she was to blame? Judd had gone off to Fort Bragg six months after Hank was born, leaving her in the house in Amesbury, Massachusetts, with his family. She had done all the washing and cooking and cleaning, and Judd had never sent a penny.

"If there is anything in the report you don't understand, we'd be glad to talk to you and your husband about it," Amy Lowery said. "You can take it with you and get back to me."

"All right," Harriet said. She stared at the woman's red-and-green-plaid dress and the white blouse under it. The woman looked Irish.

"We think Hank has problems, Mrs. Sutton. It would be best if they were addressed before he goes into the more structured first-grade classroom with boys half his size."

Harriet stood up. "Thank you," she said. "We'll read this. Thank you."

2. (1974)

"Crupper had to give me an A," Hank said loudly. "He had to. I mean, goddamn, with my slapshot, with the goals I've scored, the season I had."

"Don't swear, please," Harriet said. She was making stew in a big pot on the electric range.

Hank smiled at his father, who was sitting at the table, drinking a Coors and reading the sports page. "You see what Bobby Hull did?" Judd asked.

"Yeah, I saw. But Beliveau is better."

"Hull has a great slap shot," Judd said. "You could work on yours."

"I will," Hank said. "The thing was, Crupper couldn't have given me even a goddamn *B*."

"Don't swear," Harriet said. She glared at Hank, who leaned against the refrigerator and looked at his report card. His red hair was cut so short it looked reddish gray against his skull.

"Christ," Judd said. "I don't think I ever got better'n a C in anything. They didn't give Bs in those days, not even in phys ed. Let me see that card."

"He did a good job in music, too," Harriet said. "He made a B."

"Except I hate fucking music," Hank said. He scaled his report card across the few feet to the table.

Harriet looked at Judd, who was studying the report card. "What's this crap this guy Gardner wrote about you?" Judd asked.

"It's bullshit," Hank said.

"'Hank could do much better in history if he would pay attention,'" Judd read aloud. He laughed. "Jesus, how can you pay attention to that stuff?"

"That's what I told him," Hank said.

"What about the good-looking spic?"

"Señorita Suarez," Hank said. "She's scared of me. I should've flunked, but she gave me a C-."

"She has some body," Judd said. "Hand me another beer

from there, will you?"

Hank opened the refrigerator and handed his father a
Coors.

"Get one for yourself," Judd said. "That's for making an
A. A goddamn A. That's good work, son."

3. (1975)

UNIVERSITY OF MAINE SCOUTING REPORT
> Name: Hank Sutton
> Position: Left wing
> Height: 6'2"
> Weight: 190
> Speed: 5/10
> Strength: 9/10
> Cumulative: 83

COMMENTS: Three-year starter at Amesbury High.
Sutton led team in goals his last two seasons. Good forward
speed, excellent strength. Is solid in front of the net, but
could add 20–25 pounds and be converted to defense.
Missed two games with back spasms. No Bobby Orr, but
could be a Potvin-type if motivation is there. Or an enforcer.
(See counselor's report).

SUMMARY OR RECOMMENDATIONS: With weight
and isometric training, Sutton could gain needed toughness.
Attitude a question mark. Watch closely.

4. (1978)

"Hey, Sutton, whatziz?"
"Nothing."

"What're you doing?" Lecroix's mouth splintered into black-and-white. Teeth, and teeth missing.

"Look, Lecroix, I'm studying. What's it look like I'm doing?"

"Jerking off with a book in front of you," Lecroix said. "How about a movie?"

Hank slammed the book closed and pushed back from the desk in his chair. "No movie."

"A beer, then."

"I'm not a star, Lecroix. I have to work to keep my scholarship."

"Like you did last Sunday night, work with that old lady?"

Hank shrugged. "I don't have cheerleaders following me around. What am I supposed to do?"

"Go with me to a movie," Lecroix said. "Then we'll have some beers."

"If I don't pass this marketing test, Turner's going to bust me."

"So crib it."

"You can't crib it with Turner."

"*Mon pauvre ami,*" Lecroix said, "everybody expects us to cheat. They don't expect us to play thirty hockey games and the NCAAs unless we cheat."

"Turner will break my balls," Hank said.

"He won't catch you," Lecroix said. "Come on. It's a Nicholson movie."

5. (1979)

Hank reached across almost the width of the back porch and put out his huge hand. "Glad to meet you, Mr. Wright."

Mr. Wright's eyes narrowed toward his daughter, Beth,

who had slipped her arm inside Hank's meaty limb. "You didn't have to run off," he said. "Or did you?"

"We didn't have to," Beth said. "Not that way."

"Your mother's not taking this well. She's been to church twice since she found out."

"We went to Florida," Hank said. "And then Nassau in the Bahamas."

"We didn't mean to upset everybody," Beth said.

"We're happy," Hank said. "Isn't that enough?"

Mr. Wright looked at Hank and then at Beth. "What about school?"

"I think maybe I can get in down at Merrimac," Hank said.

"He doesn't need to finish," Beth said. "One of the alumni boosters thought Hank got a raw deal being kicked off the team. He offered him a job at Tapper Industries in Boston."

"I meant *your* school," Mr. Wright said.

"My school can wait," Beth said. "We'll have enough money . . ."

"Money helps," Mr. Wright said, "but it's not kindness."

"Hank's kind," Beth said. "He's very kind."

Mr. Wright shifted his eyes to Hank. "If you ever hurt my daughter, you'll answer to me."

6. (1983)

"You really think so?" Arnason asked. "You really think you could have made the NHL?"

There was snow on the ground outside. Arnason and Hank were sitting with colleagues in the center of the lunch-room near a large false fountain that sprayed a geyser every thirty seconds. Hank forked a slab of lasagna into his mouth.

"Hell, yes," he said, eyeing a blond from accounting across the table.

"Bullshit," Arnason said.

"I know I could have," Hank said. "There were scouts at practice all the time."

Arnason shook his head. "But quickness and all that. The pros are different animals."

"I was quick."

"I mean *release time*," Arnason said. "Vision. Size, sure. You got size in a crowd."

Hank drained his Coke, sucked it through shards of ice in the bottom of his glass. His voice came hard. "I had a heavy shot," Hank said. "They should have never switched me to defense." He paused and watched the blond spoon yogurt from her plastic cup.

"So you played in college," Arnason said. "That's different. The pros are eager. They don't go out there on the ice to dance."

"Shut up," Hank said.

"I mean, really. Gretzky—the guy has phenomenal vision. Ninety-two goals! He'd make mincemeat out of you."

"I mean *shut up*," Hank said. Without warning, he stood up and lifted Arnason, together with his chair, and carried them to the fountain, where he tipped them over the rail and into the water. Hank turned and smiled at the blond. She didn't smile back.

7. (1984–88)

Hank left his job at Tapper Industries and signed on with Inter-American Solar Dynamics in public relations. He and Beth moved from Boston to St. Louis, and, a year later, to

Denver. While he was at Inter-American, Lecroix back in Buffalo offered him a step-up at Coolidge Enterprises at fifty thousand a year. Hank took the job without giving notice.

Coolidge was a manufacturer of high-tech microdevices. Though small by industry standards, it consistently outshone the competition in research and product innovation. Long-term debt refinancing had limited its short-term performance (which had been an initial flash on the horizon), but once that problem was resolved, the company expected to resume its upward growth spiral. Price:earnings ratio was 23.4, and EPS was $.14 compared to $.43 the prior fiscal year. The current OTC quote was 3¼ to 3½.

8. (1988)

"Who is she?" Beth asked.

"Who is who?"

"The woman you're having an affair with at work."

Hank's hesitation loomed larger than the silence in the room. "I'm not having an affair."

"Dinner was three hours ago. Where have you been?"

"Gillatt took me out for a drink. He wanted to talk about the merger."

"We had guests," Beth said. "The Hollanders and Brysons were here. We waited for you."

An array of dirty glasses and dishes and tossed napkins littered the table, except at Hank's place, which was neatly set with a clean plate and silverware.

"I was terrible company," Beth said. "And they were offended. They left right after dinner. Merger? What merger? Why do you lie to me?"

Hank took his plate to the kitchen and piled it high with

potatoes and gravy and steak. "Fuck the Hollanders and Brysons," he said. "And since when have you wanted me to tell you the truth?"

9. (1989)

Winter. The bar was too noisy to discuss anything serious. Hank and his hockey friends had gotten together for a reunion in New York; they sat at a big circular table and joked with each other. The waitress had come over to take orders for another round, and Hank held the woman's arm. He pointed at Jeff Crouch, who had played on defense with him at Maine, then at Lecroix, and so on around the table. "Gin and tonic, Budweiser, Budweiser, bourbon rocks, Heineken. You got that, sweetheart?"

The woman tried to pull away from him, but Hank held her tightly.

"Whatcha doing later?" he asked.

"Let her alone, Hank," Crouch said easily.

Hank let the woman go, and she fell backward toward the bar. He laughed and drank up and looked around the crowded room. The other people were assholes. There was a bunch of dart throwers in one corner, and some stupid couples who'd obviously just been to a schmaltzy movie, and a table of flits. The air was hot and humid.

Then a black man, neatly attired in a coat and tie, appeared beside him. He said something Hank hadn't heard exactly.

"What's that?" Hank asked. He looked to Lecroix for interpretation.

"The brother says we should depart," Lecroix said.

"I'd like another beer," Hank said to the man in the white shirt. "Gin and tonic..." He pointed at Crouch. "Budweiser..."

"I think he meant it's not polite to manhandle the waitress," Lecroix said. "We're supposed to *allons-y.*"

The man in the white shirt nodded. "I'm sorry," the man said. "I hope you'll leave quietly, but if necessary I'll call the police."

Hank smiled. "That won't be necessary," Hank said. He sat forward as if to get up, and then with a convulsive roar, heaved the circular table into the air. Bottles and glasses and ice flew in every direction. Hank dropped the table on its side and lunged at the man in the white shirt.

10. (1990)

For a while after the divorce, Hank wondered whether Beth's father would come after him. He changed apartments three times, and often in the morning he checked under the hood of his car for a bomb.

One evening when he was watching TV, there was a knock on the door, and he was certain old man Wright had come for him. Hank got out his .38 special from his dresser drawer and held it to the door as he opened it.

It was Jeff Crouch in the hallway. "You are one hard mother-fucker to locate," Crouch said. He pushed at the door, but the chain was up. "Can I come in?"

"So you found me," Hank said. He took the chain off.

Crouch came inside. "What's the gun for? You all right?"

"The gun is in case someone else has one," Hank said. "You want a drink?"

"No, thanks. I got a proposition for you," Crouch said. "Do you want to listen to it? We're all a little worried about you."

"Worried how?"

Crouch wandered through the sparsely furnished living room. "You want to do some good in the world?"

"Yeah, like what?"

"A couple of afternoons a week and Saturday mornings —coach a kid's team." Crouch turned and stopped pacing. "Eleven-, twelve-year-olds. The kids would think you're a star."

Hank got out a tray of ice from the freezer and poured himself a shot of bourbon. "What's in it for me?"

"Lecroix's got a team. He'll be tough. And I've got one. We thought it'd be good for you. Come out of hiding, you know what I mean? Get back to the rink."

Hank poured more bourbon into his glass. "No, thanks," he said. "I'm real busy at work."

11. (1992)

"Card."

The Indian dealer stroked the blue-backed deck, slid the top card off, bent it and popped it over in his hand. He skidded a nine across the felt onto Hank's deuce.

"Stay," Hank said, taking another bourbon from a passing tray.

The dealer turned his cards: two queens. Hank flipped his jack.

The dealer paid one and a half on Hank's hand, waited a moment for a new player to settle in, and dealt again.

He was in a newly opened Indian-owned casino near Norwich, Connecticut.

Hank eyed his down card, a five. The dealer showed an eight. Hank's second card was a face. "Shit," he said.

"Card?"

Hank shook his head.

The dealer paired eights, had to take a hit, and busted.

"I'm hot as a two-dollar whore," Hank said, smiling and raking in his chips. He was ahead twenty-three hundred dollars.

12. (1993)

He had not seen much of his mother in several years. Occasionally she had called him in Buffalo, but when Coolidge transferred him to Connecticut she called less often. He never called her. The game of questions and answers had never meant much to him.

"How're you getting along?" she'd asked once. He'd been living outside Hartford.

"Fine."

"You going to marry this new girl?"

"She works in real estate," Hank said.

"Why don't you bring her for a visit?"

"I don't like going back to Amesbury," he said. "There's nothing there."

"I'd like to meet her. What's her name?"

"Michele."

His mother never mentioned she was sick. She didn't say that was why she called less often. She died two weeks after they'd talked.

At the funeral his father didn't cry. But when Reverend Clarkson asked in prayer for God to welcome His servant, Harriet, to the Kingdom of Heaven, Hank burst into uncontrollable sobs.

13. (1993)

MEDICAL NOTES: Dr. Hans Schumann's workup on Henry Sutton. Month 7, visit 17.

DIAGNOSIS: Moderate to severe depression, tendency toward mild schizophrenia.

TREATMENT: Reality therapy.

PROGNOSIS: Good. Mr. Sutton has worked out much of his aggression and hostility, and at least some of his suffering has been eased by his recent marriage. His heavy drinking has abated. Behavioral consequences have been modified. He has resumed his previous employment. Two further sessions are scheduled, together with follow-up.

14. (1994)

The woman walking toward him on the sidewalk looked familiar, but Hank couldn't place her. She wasn't unattractive, but not pretty, either. She stopped and smiled and said, "You're Hank Sutton."

Hank nodded.

"It isn't hard to recognize you with that red hair, no matter how long it's been. I'm Claire Green. Claire Yeager."

"Right, oh Jesus." Hank shook her hand.

"Didn't you play hockey at the university?"

"Yes, hockey," he said. "What about you?"

"I was a cheerleader." Claire's eyes moved from his face to his burgeoning stomach and back to his face again. "I'm married now and have two children. I live in West Hartford."

"I've got a little boy," Hank said. "Just born two months ago."

Claire Yeager had been beautiful in college, but this woman was not. She'd been one of Lecroix's girlfriends, sassy, with a brush-up haircut and smooth skin, a girl Hank had dreamed about. Now she was wide in the hips, and her jowls and chin drooped.

"You still look in good shape," Claire said.

"Thanks," Hank said. "I haven't slowed down much. You look good, too."

15. (1995)

The president's economic adviser predicts a major weakening of the economy . . . Hank skipped the bullshit of the interoffice memo from the Coolidge brass and read on down the page. *Reforms must be made* . . . *the field has become crowded with the introduction of* . . . *competition had become keener than anticipated* . . . *tightening of credit* . . . *fiscal condition less secure* . . . *Coolidge is experiencing decreased demand for its highest-priced line.* . .

Hank was among the first to be let go.

16. (1997)

Michele took an aerobics class Tuesday nights because she hated hockey on TV, and she was often late getting home because she went out with the girls afterward. Hank sat in his recliner with a beer cradled on his stomach. It was already 2-zip, Rangers over the Bruins—Hank hated the fucking Rangers—and the Bruins had a penalty. "Bourque is too fucking old," Hank said. "I could do a better job." He swigged on his beer.

Suddenly Brad cried in the other room.

"Fuck, now what?"

The Rangers worked the power play, passing the puck around from defenseman to the face-off circle and back. The Bruins played a pathetic box. Hank got up and got another beer.

"Shut up in there," he called to Brad, who was still crying.

He got back to the TV just as the Rangers scored. "Oh, *fuck,*" Hank said. He fell into the recliner, then got up again because Brad was screaming.

He went into the child's room just off the hallway. "Now what the hell is the matter with you?"

Brad was sitting up in bed and squinted into the light shining from the living room. He stopped crying.

"What's the damned trouble?" Hank asked.

"I want the light on."

"You know the rules. No light."

"Where's Mommy?"

"She's not here."

The crowd roared on the TV in the living room, and Hank closed the door hard. He ran back to catch the replay. A fight had broken out—a Bruin had bumped the precious Ranger goalie, and there was a major brawl.

Brad shrieked.

"Quiet in there," Hank called. He drank a long swallow of beer.

The referees separated the last two fighters, and order was restored. Penalties were handed out, an extra one to the Bruins. Hank was livid. "What the hey?" he said. "Make them even . . ."

Brad's crying shot right through the closed door. Hank gulped his beer and set the bottle down just as Brad opened the door and appeared in the hallway.

"Daddy?"

"Get back in bed."

The boy's face was red, his cheeks shiny with tears. His eyes were slitted to the light.

"Do as you're told."

"I want Mommy."

"To hell with your mother. Get back in bed."

"Can I have the light on?"

Hank glared at Brad and stood up, and the boy began to wail again. In three steps Hank was across the room and caught Brad's wrist and yanked him off the ground. He carried him by his one arm to the doorway and slapped his behind. "Now you get in *bed!*"

He threw the boy toward the bed, but too hard, and Brad skipped off the bed and hit the table on the other side. His water spilled and the lamp fell over. Brad's crying stopped abruptly.

"Brad, goddamn it, *listen*. You have to listen when I tell you to do something."

Hank went around the bed and picked the boy up gently and laid him on the sheets. Brad's arms and legs began to twitch and quiver violently.

"Brad?"

Hank picked him up again and rushed out into the living room where the TV still blared away. Hank took the stairs in twos down to the carport. The Jeep Cherokee, bought on time, was eerie in the phosphorescent light from the street. He pushed Brad into the passenger seat. The boy's eyes were closed; the shaking had stopped. Then Hank ran around and climbed in and started the engine.

At the corner he ran the stop sign, then careened past a slow-moving Dodge onto the boulevard. "*Drive,*" he shouted. "You ass, get out of the way!"

Then he was on Interstate 84. Lights flashed by like small explosions. He passed car after car at eighty, eighty-five. Two exits went by. Then another. He kept shaking his head, driving faster, blindly, and tears welled up from a terrible empty space within him.

ALTON'S KEEPER

THE SQUASH COURT IN CHARLESTON WAS IN A RUN-DOWN neighborhood off East Bay Street across from the Sea-Land storage depot. A Princeton alumnus had built it in the back of his warehouse, and though he no longer played himself, he let those of us use it who were brave enough to venture into the black projects. In 1980 squash was still a Yankee game practiced by rich boys in Ivy League schools, but those of us in the South who'd picked up the game were fanatics.

On one particular Saturday in mid-April, Will Fordham, my doctor friend, and I had just endured a grueling five-game match and were sitting outside on the loading dock, having a beer and enjoying the sea breeze sliding from the harbor. Behind the warehouse, children yelled and basketballs thumped on the playground, and across the vacant lot, a black woman was hanging laundry on the second-story porch of an old wooden house. The topic of conversation was Will's sister-in-law Rachel, who was moving down from Spartanburg. Will's wife, Sarah, wanted to introduce her to Charleston society at the upcoming Yacht Club dance, and my cooperation was being earnestly solicited. "Good legs," Will said, "and not a bad face, either. And bazooms . . ." He held his hands cupped in front of his sweaty T-shirt. "She's a fine girl, Tom."

"You don't make her sound like a fine girl."

"We could all go to the dance together," Will said.

"I may have to go to my needlepoint class," I said.

Will laughed. "After all Sarah has done for you?"

I was rescued for the moment by a rattletrap Toyota Corolla station wagon that careened around the corner. The brakes squealed, and it veered into the parking lot. The car was dusty and crammed with camping gear, boxes of food, and photo equipment—a tripod protruded from the open back window. Will and I knew who it was: Alton Maddox.

Alton turned off the engine and creaked open the driver's door. "Thirty-one hours from Big Bend, Texas," he said. "Anyone want to play squash?"

Alton hadn't shaved in days, and the sunburned skin around his eyes was crinkled with tiny white lines. He looked exhausted and a little crazed, a zombie.

"What were you doing in Big Bend?" Will asked.

"Photographing hummingbirds," he said. "I got the Lucifer."

"Maybe Alton should take Rachel to the dance," I said. "He'd fit in at the Yacht Club."

"Are you still married?" Will asked him.

"That depends," Alton said. "Who's Rachel?"

"According to Will, Rachel is the perfect woman."

"Yes, but doctors only know imperfection." Alton uncoiled from the seat, stood up, and stretched. "A dollar a game," he said. "I'll give the victim six points."

Then suddenly he reached back through the window of his car and retrieved his camera. "Hold still," he said. He took off the lens cap and pointed the Nikon at Will.

"What are you doing?" Will asked.

Alton clicked a few pictures, then turned the camera on me.

I never liked being photographed—something about losing the soul—and I lifted my hands in front of my face. Alton clicked several pictures anyway. Then he wheeled around to the vacant lot and squeezed off several more shots in the direction of the dilapidated house where clothes luffed in the breeze.

Finally he stopped and lowered the camera. "Last of the film," he said. "Come on, Tom, I'll play you a few games for free."

The Monday after, Alton's wife, Clarice, called me at my office. She was from a wealthy plantation family and had studied cello in New York, and I'd always equated her with that instrument—whiny, self-absorbed, able to make something somber of any note. "Have you seen him, Tom?" she asked. "I know he's in town."

"He beat me in squash on Saturday," I said. "I haven't seen him since then."

"He hasn't come home," Clarice said. "He couldn't have disappeared. You don't know where he is?"

"I'm not his keeper," I said.

"But you're his friend."

Clarice's asking me to find Alton was an order, and I pondered where Alton might go—what bars he went to, what people he knew. When he was in town, I played squash with him, but I didn't know him well. Not like I knew Will, from childhood. Alton was an odd mix of serious and funny, intelligence and antic risk. After squash he bolted without saying a word, or he might drink a six-pack and urge Will and me to go out and eat oysters and drink tequila shots. He talked of strange things: birds, meditation, how to live without money. He was not one of us, really, not from here.

After lunch I drove around to the squash court. Alton sometimes played at that hour, and his Toyota was there. I found him inside heating mushroom soup on a campstove.

"What the hell are you doing?" I asked.

"Having lunch," he said. "You want some soup?"

His foam pad and sleeping bag were rolled out on the

court. He stirred the soup and spooned some from the pan to his mouth.

"Why aren't you home?" I asked.

"I couldn't go back, Tom. I drove all those miles and it was clear Clarice never loved me."

"Of course she loves you," I said. "You're *married.*"

"You think that explains something?" he asked.

"Look, Alton, you can't live here."

"I roll up my sleeping bag when someone wants to play. There's a toilet and a shower."

"What about your house? Your darkroom?"

"This place is black when you turn out the lights."

I struggled for purchase. How could I argue with Alton? "What about her money?" I asked.

Alton spooned a few more mouthfuls of soup. "I don't *take* her money," he said. He looked at me. "You don't know what love is, do you, Tom?"

"I know there are different kinds of love."

Alton smiled. "Well, that's a start." He poured a cup of soup and held it out to me.

I hesitated, as if I knew eating lunch with Alton was a mistake. Then I took the soup and sat down on the floor.

As Will said, I owed Sarah Fordham for several favors she'd done me, not the least of which was letting me stay in her carriage house back in the fall before I found a place to live. Taking Rachel to the dance was a sentence I accepted, if not willingly, then bravely. Still, the evening loomed like darkness on the horizon.

By Charleston standards, my family was moderately well off. We didn't have the money Clarice's family did, or Will's. My father sold houses and played golf, and my mother was a French professor at the college. They owned a white house shaded by live oaks on Church Street, and they had enough to send me to Porter-Gaud School and to the University of Virginia. I'd had a fellowship to Penn graduate school for a year (where I'd learned squash), but I'd dropped out and worked in a bank in Atlanta for two years. I didn't much like Atlanta—too glitzy—and when my father offered me a job, I came back to Charleston and the grand old houses on the Battery, the sea air and palm trees, the women selling gladioluses across from the Episcopal church.

The bungalow I'd rented on Legare Street was within walking distance of the office. It was two bedrooms upstairs, a small living room/dining room/kitchen downstairs, a worn brick path to the door. I took an interest in the garden. Azaleas of mauve and white bloomed along the side porch, and I cultivated nasturtiums, gladioluses, even roses. My friends from the old days came by—Will and Sarah, the mayor's son Duke Maxwell and his wife Penny, and Grayson Worth of Worth Gardens. We sat on the porch and drank bourbon under the slow-moving ceiling fan.

Now was the time to act: that was the consensus. Air-conditioning had made the South bearable, and Northerners who'd suffered all their lives in the cold had driven up property values. Grayson had lopped off part of his gardens for an exclusive development with a golf course; Duke and Penny were leveraging stocks to invest in rental properties.

All this was good news to me. "That's what I came back for," I said. "To make money."

"And marry a pretty girl," Sarah said. "Tom, you're dangerous as a single man."

Everyone laughed; I was as dangerous as a flower.

But the first few months home weren't what I'd hoped for, either in the romance department or in my father's office. My father believed in house sales, and that was that.

"Six percent is not a way to get rich," I said.

We were in the drawing room on Church Street, drinking brandy.

"It is if you sell enough houses."

"The South is joining the modern world. Now's the time to cash in."

My father drank his brandy slowly, the way he did everything. He was a slender man, gray hair neatly trimmed, well dressed. He wore beige slacks and a blue blazer. Appearances meant something to him. "We're doing all right," he said. "What's your hurry?" He put his snifter down on the coffee table. "What would you do to change the world?"

"Develop commercial property. Convert warehouses to office space, acquire run-down buildings and refurbish . . ."

"Do people live in such places?"

"The Germans and Japanese have a balance-of-payments glut. They're looking to invest."

"You want the Japanese owning Charleston?"

"What does it matter?" I said. "In two thousand years the earth will be a frozen snowball."

"Then let's keep it as it is as long as we can." He studied me and sighed. Then he surprised me. "You bring me a proposal," he said, "and we'll talk."

The next week I talked to Grayson Worth. He knew of a small shopping center that might come on the market. The owner's wife had died and he wanted to be near his daughter in Florida, but he hadn't decided yet to sell. I drove across the Cooper River Bridge to Mount Pleasant to look at it.

It was a dozen stores—shoe store, pet supply, frame shop, a Chinese restaurant—built in the 1960s, not in good condition. The bypass didn't help, either. Through traffic raced past at fifty miles an hour, cut off from the frontage road. But things could be changed.

On the way back over the bridge, I opened the sunroof of the Saab and called my secretary, Ann Lowell, on the car phone. "Your father wants to know if you've made progress on the Harboldt listing," she said.

"Zero."

"And Mrs. Fordham called. She invited you for cocktails before the dance. I picked up your tuxedo."

"Thank you, Ann. Anything else?"

"Alton Maddox wants you to play squash at five."

It was four-thirty then, and I clicked off the phone and ascended the arc of the bridge. Below me the peninsula of the city was surrounded by a glittering sea. I saw the billowing live oaks, the houses on the Battery, the white steeple of St. Michael's, and as I crested the bridge, I had a clear vision of the future. With the profit from the shopping center, I'd start my own development company. I'd meet a woman—maybe Rachel—and fall instantly in love. We'd buy a house on Tradd Street. All this would thread into the perfect tapestry.

At the bottom of the bridge I turned onto East Bay. On the left were warehouses and shipping storage depots, and on the right, the brick projects interspersed with run-down houses. I drove to Charlotte Street, where the squash court was, and pulled into the parking lot.

Alton's car wasn't there, but I took him at his word and went in to change.

His camping gear was piled in a corner of the dressing area, and in the bathroom were several dozen photographs hanging on wires. I put on my shorts and tennis shoes and my sweaty shirt and then was curious about the pictures. There were delicate close-ups of hummingbirds feeding at cactus flowers, and the ones he had taken of Will and me a couple of weeks earlier. Will had the weary, carefree expression of his best moments, when he wasn't thinking of social graces or medicine, but the ones of me were silly. My hands were in front of my face, but my expression was still visible: I came across as vain and juvenile, perhaps arrogant.

The other photographs—six or seven in all—were collages of vivid and oddly compatible colors composed almost like paintings. I took several of them down and held them in better light. The colors were clothes—a maroon dress, two yellow blouses, a pink sheet, a pair of women's blue underwear. There was a partial figure in each of them—part of a dark shoulder, two black fingers pinning the pink sheet, a forehead and black hair obscured by a yellow blouse. Only one photo showed the black woman's whole face and upper body. She was in her late twenties and had on a blue sundress with a strap loose over one shoulder. Her face bore directly into the wind because her hair was blown back, and she gazed toward the harbor as if there were something in the distance she couldn't make out. In that attitude of unawareness—in that *instant* Alton created her—she struck me as the most beautiful woman I had ever seen.

I went into the squash court and warmed up the ball hitting it against the wall. After a few minutes, though, when Alton hadn't shown up, I got dressed again and left him a note.

> I can't play. If you need a place to stay
> for a few days, let me know.
>   Tom

I left the note tucked in the door jamb.

That night I had dreams I couldn't remember. I woke in a sweat and lay shivering under the covers. When it was light, I got up and walked downtown to St. Cecelia's, a gentleman's club off Broad Street, where I frequently had breakfast. George, the maitre d', greeted me and led me to a table by the window.

"You're up early this morning, Mr. Pritchett," he said.

He pulled out the chair for me under an ornate chandelier and put a menu at my place. But I didn't sit down. I looked around at the other tables, all empty at that hour, their white tablecloths with plates and silverware and crystal glasses neatly arranged.

"Can I ask you something, George?"

"I may not know the answer," George said.

"How old is the club?"

"Founded 1783."

"And how long have you worked here?"

"Me? Oh, not since then." He laughed out loud and pulled the chair out another inch or two.

"How long?"

"About twenty years."

"Has there ever been a black person in here?"

George's jocular manner vanished, and he furrowed his white brow. "The waiters," he said. "The cook."

"You know what I mean—to sit at a table and eat."

"I don't work every meal, Mr. Pritchett."

"Thanks, George," I said, and I sat down.

Several days later, between showing houses, I called the owner of the shopping center in Mount Pleasant. He hadn't got as far as a price, but he was glad of my interest. If he sold he wanted it quick and easy. A deal was a deal, he said. No brokers or middlemen.

I took from his tone and manner enough encouragement to call Duke Maxwell, who was connected to people in the mayor's office and on the zoning commission. With the right information and persuasion, the commission might grant a variance for a new access off the bypass. After that, a traffic light would be mandatory. A few contractors met me at the shopping center to give me ideas for remodeling the shops.

When I'd done the fundamental research, I took my father to lunch at Henry's Seafood. I laid out the plat maps and several photographs. "Is the Chinese restaurant any good?" he asked.

"I've never eaten there."

"It matters," he said. "A restaurant draws people. Have you talked to the store owners?"

"Not yet."

"They'll be paying increased rents."

"But they'll also get more customers."

The oysters arrived, a dozen on the half shell. We each took one and dipped it in butter.

"This may surprise you, Tom, but some people don't want more customers." My father slid the oyster into his mouth.

"Since when?" I asked.

"The store owners may already have enough work. They may not be able to cope with hiring new people in order to expand. Maybe they're happy as they are."

"Like you?" I said.

He paused, and I glimpsed something just for a brief second beyond the veneer of his suit and tie. He quickly covered it over. "Yes," he said. "Like me."

On Saturday evening I appeared at Will and Sarah's house on Gibbes Street a little before six. Sarah greeted me in the foyer. She looked fresh, if not pretty, in her lilac dress with a white sash around her waist, and her hair was done up in a French twist. Her makeup was darker than usual around the eyes and redder on the lips, which distracted one's attention from her nose and overlarge ears. "Rachel isn't ready yet," she said. "Will you pour me a Dubonnet?"

"I'd be glad to," I said. "Where's Will?"

"Shining his shoes. Are you nervous?"

"A little."

We went into the living room, and Sarah pulled the curtains across the sunlight. I poured a Dubonnet and a strong vodka tonic.

"Have you talked to Alton lately?" she asked.

I gave her her glass, then took a long sip from mine. "Not for a while. Why?"

"Clarice has filed for divorce."

"Clarice exaggerates."

"How can you exaggerate a divorce? Will thinks Alton is evil."

"Because he takes pictures of birds?"

"We can call evil whatever we choose," Sarah said.

Footsteps echoed along the wooden floor in the hallway, and Rachel came in. She wore a pale pink gown with white lace at the sleeves and pearls around her neck. She was taller and prettier than Sarah, more refined looking. Her face appeared sculpted, the skin smooth across the cheekbones, her nose delicate. She lifted a hand to her dark brown hair, as if she were not used to its being permed. Then she sniffed her wrist. "My God, I smell like an orchid."

She raised her generous eyes to mine, and I forgot Alton Maddox and the shopping center and that Sarah was in the room.

The dance was in the ballroom at the Yacht Club on the Lower Battery. A half-dozen chandeliers illuminated the dance floor, and long, brocaded drapes framed the high doorways to the outside veranda, which overlooked the marina. A light from Fort Sumter flashed across the water from the darkness.

Most of the men wore black tuxedos, though here and there, sprinkled among the bankers and lawyers and doctors, was someone in a white or maroon coat. The women were painted birds dressed in pastels. Their full skirts floated to the orchestra music, and their smiles gave the impression that nothing bad could happen on such an evening—or ever.

Rachel and I drank champagne, made small talk, and danced. She rested in my arms and followed expertly and smoothly. At certain moments—when we went out on the terrace to look at the boats, or at the end of a waltz when we lingered after the last note—each of us was attuned to the other in an almost mystical way. My parents, at a table not far away, smiled their approval. Already I was thinking of houses I knew were for sale on Tradd Street.

At ten o'clock the orchestra took a break, and Sarah and Rachel went to the ladies' room. Will came over and sat down beside me.

"I told you she had a good body," he said.

"That's not a fundamental requirement."

"She has money, too."

"I like her," I said.

A scuffle at the entrance drew our attention. Voices rose and fell, and along with other guests, Will and I stood up to see what the commotion was. Suddenly Alton Maddox emerged from the crowd onto the empty dance floor. He had on jeans and a T-shirt and was holding the hand of the black woman I'd seen in the photograph. She was dressed as casually as Alton—in shorts and a yellow blouse and sneakers. I'd have thought she'd be intimidated by the crowd, but her expression was neither challenging nor scared. She looked completely at ease.

Alton turned a slow circle in the middle of the floor. "Tom Pritchett," he called. "Where are you, Tom?"

"That bastard," Will said. "What's he doing?"

Sarah and Rachel slipped back to the table beside us. "Isn't that Alton?" Sarah asked.

"He must be drunk," Will said.

"Tom Pritchett?" Alton said. "Talk to me, Tom."

The orchestra came back and took their places at the bandstand, but they didn't play.

"Who is it?" Rachel asked.

Sarah leaned close to me. "Now do you think he's evil?"

Alton turned around in a full circle, his hands out in supplication. "You said I could stay with you, Tom. I need the key to your house."

I took a half step forward, but Will held my arm. "Keep quiet," Will said. "The stewards will get rid of him."

But my half step caught the black woman's attention. She looked at me and nudged Alton. Alton smiled. "Tom," he said.

Then the orchestra started playing a samba—horns, a snare, mariachis. Two stewards and a policeman strode onto the dance floor. Alton held my gaze, as if he were asking me something. Then the black woman pushed him toward the open terrace. They ran. Couples got up to dance, and in a few seconds the society of Charleston whirled across the floor as if Alton and the black woman had never been there.

At St. Cecelia's Monday morning, people talked about the embarrassment Alton had caused me and my parents, not to mention Clarice. In the lobby after breakfast, I ran into Duke Maxwell. He wanted to know who Alton Maddox was and whether it was true I had offered him a place to stay. I said yes, but in another context, not the evening of the dance.

No one asked the real question, except my father.

I went to see him that morning about the Harboldt listing. We'd had an offer, but ridiculously low. My father didn't care about that. Instead, he asked, "What was he doing with her, that friend of yours?"

"He met her at the squash court," I said. "He took some photographs of her."

"Things like that can hurt you, Tom. Do you see that? They

can hurt me. Ben Hartnett at First Federal already called me."

"About what?"

"In this business everything has consequences," my father said.

"Well," I said, "it shouldn't. All I did was offer—"

"I didn't say it should. I said it does. Are you listening to me?"

"Yes, I'm listening," I said.

In early June I closed on the Harboldt house. The firm made $12,600, which did not cover overhead for the month. My father claimed we earned an equal amount of goodwill, but dealing with Mrs. Harboldt had required every ounce of my tact.

Meanwhile, Pritchett Associates—my father and I as a separate partnership—signed a contract to purchase the Lanier Shopping Center, contingent upon financing. My father golfed with several bank executives so we had an inside track on a loan, but he avoided doing anything. Finally I cornered him in his office. "We have a June thirtieth contract deadline," I said. "I'd like to schedule the contractors, but I can't until we get the loan approved."

"I'm concerned about the merchants," he said.

"We have to expect resistance. No one likes change."

"Resistance is different from lawsuits."

"The sooner we're in, the sooner we're out."

"The fast buck," my father said. "That's what made America what it is today."

During these weeks, I saw Rachel when we could schedule our evenings together. She was between places, getting packed to move from Spartanburg and looking for a job in Charleston. We went to a few new movies—*Ordinary People* and *Melvin and Howard*—to dinner at the Chinese restaurant (good egg rolls and sweet-and-sour pork), once to Magnolia Gardens to see the azaleas and camellias still blooming. When we walked together, she took my arm, and at the end of the evening, she kissed me good night.

Then on a Saturday I took her sailing on my parents' yawl. Rachel had fixed a picnic basket, and I'd brought two six-packs of Heineken in a red cooler. Rachel had done her hair in a ponytail and wore cutoffs and a jacket over a striped shirt. She'd brought a sketchbook; I hadn't known she was an artist.

We motored past the jetty, and while Rachel kept us into the wind, I raised the main and the jib. We tacked northeastward along the barrier islands and, after a couple of hours, came inshore to have lunch in the lee of Bull Island. The Worths— Grayson's parents—were on a forty-foot sloop in the cut between the islands, and I recognized Ben Hartnett from the bank strolling on the beach with his grandchildren. I threw the anchor and coiled the lines, then came aft for a Heineken.

Rachel was drawing. She'd stripped off her shirt and the top of her bikini and was concentrating on some point on the island. She must have heard me, but she didn't turn. "The sun feels so good," she said.

Her breasts were large, as Will had said, dark-tipped. She hadn't been much in the sun because her skin was pale and without lines. "What are you doing?" I asked.

"Sketching the island."

"I mean there are other people around."

Rachel glanced at the Worths' sloop. "They don't care about us." She looked at me. "Don't you like my body?"

"That's not the issue." I took off my shirt and threw it to her. "Everything has consequences."

She did not put the shirt on. Instead, she stood up on the deck and stretched languidly, as if she didn't care what I thought or who saw her.

"Is that what kept you silent at the dance?" she asked.

"What?"

"You're afraid to be seen?"

I didn't answer, and she threw my shirt back at me. Then she climbed to the rail and dived into the water.

My father co-signed the note, and we closed on the shopping center. I hired contractors, carpenters, painters, a paving company for the parking lot. Several shopkeepers rebelled, and I spent hours in meetings with them and their lawyers. I was so busy I didn't have time or energy to see Rachel or to play squash.

To unwind, I took long walks at night. At first I strolled the neighborhood around Legare Street as far as the town houses at Colonial Lake. Then gradually I walked farther afield. One night I walked down Calhoun to King Street and turned north, past the public library and into the seedy area of thrift stores, furniture showrooms, and pawn shops. Black men drinking from paper bags lounged on the sidewalks and on the stoops. Once a black woman shouted at me from a passing car, and another time someone threw an empty beer can that caromed off a telephone pole and rolled into the gutter. I didn't know what I was doing in that part of town—I'd never done more than drive through it—but it seemed important to me to be there. At the Piggly Wiggly near the overpass, I turned onto Spring Street and into a section of run-down houses. I bore right on America Street, past boarded-up shacks with dark windows and overgrown yards, and right again on East Bay, toward downtown.

The Seaman's Bar and the dockworkers' union hall gave way to warehouses, and I detoured a block off East Bay to see whether Alton's car might still be at the squash court. I thought maybe he'd headed west again. But his car was there, and a line of light shone under the door of the warehouse.

It was eleven o'clock. The muffled thump of the squash ball ricocheting off the wall came through the door, and I unlocked it, and pushed it open quietly. Voices. The ball thudded against the walls, the *whap* of racquets. Laughing. A woman's voice. I waited till the ball was in play and climbed the metal stairs to the gallery.

Alton was one of the players, of course, and if I'd guessed the other, I'd have been right. Still, seeing the black woman surprised me. She was adept with the racquet, agile moving around the court. Now and then Alton exhorted her with a word or two—"Move up," or "Stretch, don't run"—but mostly each moved the other in gentle choreography to the side of the court, then stepped around to the tee.

I watched as long as I dared. During a rally, I retreated down the ladder and went outside. I walked several paces to the empty playground nearby, shaking uncontrollably. Then I did something odd: I shouted out into the darkness. *AAAH!* A long, brutal cry. I didn't know what it meant. I felt the wind off the water, heard the traffic skim on the pavement on the Cooper River Bridge, looked up at the sky and the stars. I raised my arms and turned a full circle beneath the scattered black windows of the warehouses.

Then I ran. The streets were empty at that hour, and I ran blindly, without knowing where I was, until I turned on Calhoun and, several blocks distant, saw the familiar white spire of St. Michael's illuminating the night sky.

On a warm evening later that week, in the midst of pouring his ritual shot of Dickel before dinner, my father complained of chest pains. Will came over right away and examined him, and afterward we went outside where my mother was sitting under the live oak on a white-painted wrought-iron chair.

"Angina," Will said, "but to be safe, I want him to have some tests at the hospital tomorrow. He should take it easy for a while."

"Maybe he was worried about the debt on the shopping center," I said.

My mother looked at me. "Your father doesn't worry," she said. "He does what he wants. And so do you." She got up and walked off into the garden.

I was puzzled by her anger and turned to Will. "I'm sorry," I said.

"It's not your fault, Tom."

I walked out with him through the iron gate to the sidewalk. The pink and blue pastel houses along Church Street shone with an eerie glow of late sun, and the shadows of palm trees cut jagged patterns across the facades. A violin, a real one, was playing Brahms. The music floated in the humid air and resonated in me in a way that was not at all peaceful.

Will unlocked his BMW at the curb. "Angina is serious," he said.

"I know."

He looked at me. "Is something wrong, Tom? I mean, other than your father's illness?"

"Like what?"

"You've been behaving strangely lately. Rachel mentioned it, too."

"I haven't seen Rachel in days."

"Do you want to talk about it?"

I looked for the music. It was all around me in the air, but there was no open window I could see. "I don't think I could," I said.

"We've been friends a long time," Will said.

"That's why," I said. "Don't you see? You're the last person I could tell."

Will looked at me with practiced sympathy. Mercifully the violin stopped, and I smiled, but it was a false smile. Will thought he understood, and he smiled back and, thinking he was respecting my silence, got into his car.

I was watching the news on the miniature television on my kitchen counter when there was a knock on the door. It was late, past ten, and I looked out the window and saw Alton on the lawn doing jumping jacks. Light and shadow scattered from the street lamp through the live oak. He saw me, too, but he didn't stop.

I opened the door, and the black woman was there on the doorstep. "I'm Yolanda," she said, and she put out her hand. She had on the same blue sundress as in the photograph.

I took her hand—I didn't know what else to do—and Alton stopped the jumping jacks and came over. "Can we come in?" he asked.

I opened the door wider, and they came into the kitchen. I turned off the television. "It's late for a visit," I said.

Alton and Yolanda looked at one another, as if deciding who should speak.

"What is it?" I asked.

"I have an assignment to photograph ptarmigan in Colorado," he said. "I don't know how long I'll be gone."

"My mother has to move from her house by the squash court," Yolanda said.

I had trouble following what they were saying.

"They're going to build a high-rise," Alton said, "with a view of the harbor."

"The squash court will go, too," Yolanda said.

"She needs a place to stay, Tom."

"Yolanda's mother needs a place to stay," I said.

"She's going to move in with her sister," Alton said. "It's

Yolanda we're talking about."

"Why doesn't she go with you?" I asked.

"Her job is here," Alton said. "She's a nurse."

There was a sudden, long silence. In that silence I understood what they were asking, and I averted my gaze and
looked into the yard. At the edge of the lawn the late-blooming
pink and white azaleas were small stars in the night. The live
oak shimmered in the street light. But what I saw in the window was myself—a reflection gray and shadowy and broken.

"For how long?" I asked. "Can't I think about it?"

"What's there to think about?" Alton said. "Either you're
willing, or you're not."

"He's not," Yolanda said.

I glanced away from my own reflection in the window and
saw hers.

Yolanda was a private nurse for a terminally ill woman who
lived on Beaufain Street. Every morning I heard Yolanda's
alarm go off, and I waited in bed until she was gone. Then I got
up and showered and shaved and went out for breakfast. Not
wanting to see my father's friends, I stopped going to St.
Cecelia's and instead walked to a diner on Meeting Street. I
had lunch there, too, and dinner out, or at my parents'.

My father was doing better, though his recovery fueled a
new silence. He ate quietly, asking only for gravy or pepper
or a second helping of red rice. He didn't want to know what
was happening at the office or with the shopping center.
Some-times I thought he was on the verge of speaking to me,
as if he had decided on some course of action, but it was still
not fixed sufficiently in his mind, for after dinner he went off
to his study alone.

At night I continued my long walks—each night through a
different part of town—and often on my way home, I walked

by Yolanda's mother's old house and the vacant lot and the squash court in the warehouse to see what changes had been wrought in the neighborhood. A house here and there had been torn down, a street closed, a storage depot cleaned up of pipe and cement blocks. Alton's car was gone.

I returned home late, after Yolanda was in bed. In the kitchen, the sink and counters and stove were clean, but the scent of her meal lingered there. Her red-and-gold purse was on the chair; her beige jacket hung on the hook beside the door. The lights upstairs were off, and when I climbed the stairs to my room, I felt the dampness in the air from her shower. The door to her room was ajar, and I paused there at the thin sliver of darkness and listened to her breathing.

Three weeks went by like that. I showed houses, closed on two my father had under contract, listed several more. I went around to the shopping center: the paving contractor had delays getting permits; I had to call Duke Maxwell. The sewing shop and the pet supply store went out of business rather than pay higher rent, and it took a week and several meetings to find new lessees. A broker in Dallas called and said he had a French syndicate looking for investment property in the South.

One Saturday afternoon I stopped by the house after an agents' tour. Yolanda worked Saturdays, too, and I didn't think she'd be there, but she was—digging a hole in the corner of the yard for a magnolia sapling. She had on jeans and a white cotton blouse, and she was sweating.

She stopped digging. "What are you doing here?" she asked. "I thought you were a ghost who came only at night."

"I've been busy," I said.

"People are moving," she said. "That's for sure." She looked at my long-neglected gladioluses. "You should weed your garden once in a while."

I bent down and plucked a few weeds, and Yolanda went on digging.

Then she said, "Your mother was here."

"What did she want?"

Yolanda stopped digging again and kneeled down. She set the magnolia tree into the hole and untied the burlap around the roots. "She thought I was your gardener," Yolanda said.

"And what did you say?"

"I said I lived here."

"And what did she say to that?"

"She asked my name. Then she said she needed to talk to you about your father. He wants to go to Alaska."

Yolanda poured water from a pail into the hole, then scooped earth with her hands in around the sapling. She stood up and pressed the earth with her shoe. "I hope you don't mind that I'm planting this tree."

I shook my head. "What's he want to go to Alaska for?"

"Your mother said he wants to see a moose."

"A moose?" I turned away and walked across the lawn. "My father is not a traveler. My mother dragged him to Paris once, and he hated it."

"And a grizzly bear," Yolanda said.

"Jesus," I said.

Yolanda kneeled again by the magnolia tree and bowed her head, and for the first time since I'd come into the yard, I was conscious of her. Yes, I had been aware of her body, her presence, her being there. I had watched her plant the tree. But suddenly I realized she had been planting the tree for a reason, that beyond the moment she was feeling something.

I crossed the lawn and stood behind her for a moment, and then I kneeled down beside her.

"Mrs. Stein died this morning," she said. "She was old

and sick and she had a good life. She knew John Kennedy. But that didn't save her. I took care of her for three years."

Yolanda looked at me. Tears were in her eyes, but she didn't cry. I wanted to hold her, but I couldn't.

My father planned to cruise up the Inland Passage to Glacier Bay, take a bus to Anchorage, then a train to Denali Park. "Moose, grizzly bears, caribou, maybe a wolf," he said. "Then I'm going to Kenya to see the beasts of Africa."

We were outside on the terrace on the second floor, standing at the railing.

My mother sat on the wicker chair. "What do you think of this, Tom?" my mother asked. "Your father's as crazy as you are."

"I'm not crazy," my father said.

"You're supposed to take it easy," she said. "Rest, play golf."

"I hate golf," my father said. "I'm bored. I've been bored since the day we got married."

"Now you tell me," she said. "I have a son who lives with a black woman, and a husband who hates me."

She got up and disappeared inside.

"I want to see a snow leopard," my father said. "A Bengal tiger."

"As I remember it, you don't like to travel," I said.

"I'll have to learn," he said.

My father went inside to his desk and came back with his briefcase. He opened it and sat down in the wicker chair, then sorted through some papers. "I've been to my lawyer, Tom. These are all in order." He handed me a sheaf of papers. "Even if the shopping center loses money, you'll have a source of income."

I read the first few lines of the first page. "You're selling me the business?"

"I'll get an annuity."

"Dad, I don't want the business."

My father looked confused. "You can take whatever risks you want," he said. "That's your objection, isn't it? I'm too conservative." My father stood and walked to the balcony. "All my life I thought you'd come back home and take over the business," he said. "I thought . . . but it doesn't matter what I thought."

"I don't want to sell houses," I said.

"Neither do I," he said.

I stood up and put my arm over his shoulder and hugged him. It was an awkward gesture, and he tensed up, but I held him anyway. I couldn't explain what I felt in any other way.

The next day I canceled my afternoon appointments and took the yawl out alone. The weather was warm and breezy, and in the harbor I hoisted the main. The offshore wind carried me quickly out beyond the shipping channel to open water.

The boat was not too big for one man in no hurry to go anywhere. I wanted to feel the boat lean, to understand the motion of the air, to sense the land dissipating behind me. Trees blurred into buildings. The city's skyline—the great houses along the Battery—faded into the hazy heat. Then there was nothing. I kept my course east away from the mounting clouds and the sunshafts that bore down through them. The sky paled. Stars came out overhead, but to the west, in the distance, thunder rolled, and lightning hovered in the clouds. I don't know how long I sailed east. The wind was steady, and I felt the eerie calm of action—waves and sky and being out beyond all reasonable limits.

When the storm overtook me, I came about and headed into it, and for an hour the boat heaved and pitched, and I was soaked in salt spray and rain. But I wasn't afraid. The storm passed, and the sky cleared again. The lights of an ocean liner moved slowly across the horizon.

Not long after that I turned back and tacked west.

The early light came from behind me like a ghost, and the beacon of the lighthouse on Sullivan's Island whirled at intervals across the sea. Land re-formed itself in dark patches on the horizon. I wished for a new world undiscovered, where property was not bought and sold or spoken for, where no houses stood, and power was a word with no meaning. But the city took its appointed shape—the Battery, the steeple of St. Michael's. A diffusion of lights from the dark continent glowed dully against the sky.

The French syndicate came in with a too-generous offer, almost site-unseen, as it were, and I met with my attorney a dozen times, made three trips to Atlanta, and was on the telephone for hours. I reduced my office time and turned over my closings to an associate eager to please.

It was during this interval that Alton called from a pay phone in Colorado. He'd finished his assignment, but had accepted a new one following the Whooping Cranes on their migration north. "How are you and Yolanda getting along?" he asked.

"Fine, but I'm concerned about her."

"In what way?"

"She hasn't worked lately. Mrs. Stein died, and she hasn't found anyone else."

"She's had offers?"

"Yes."

"Give her time," Alton said.

There was a pause on the line. A recorded voice asked for more money.

"Hello?" Alton said.

"I don't know what will happen," I said.

"What do you mean?"

"I mean, in her *life*," I said. "She's . . ." I didn't know what to say.

"Listen to you," Alton said.

"What?"

"Just *listen*," he said.

The pay phone beeped again. "I have to go," Alton said. "Good-bye, Tom."

And he was gone.

On the afternoon I closed on the sale of the shopping center, Yolanda wasn't home, and I sat in the garden. The neighbor next door was edging her lawn, and across the street a painter freshened the blue shutters on Anna Bibra's house. The sky was low and hot and gray. Rain seemed imminent. A mockingbird sang in the tree above me.

The azaleas were gone then; so were the gladioluses. It was August, and the greenness without flowers disturbed me. My father and I had each made a third of a million dollars, but the anticipated elation never materialized. Instead I felt relieved. I was glad to be out of the deal.

I got up and picked up the hoe leaning against the porch and scratched at the ground. I dug around the azaleas, made a dry moat for the magnolia sapling Yolanda had planted, turned the earth under the rose trellis. I worked until I felt blisters starting on my hands.

When I put the hoe back, Yolanda was standing on the brick walk. "They're tearing down the warehouse tomorrow," she said. "Do you want to play squash one last time?"

It began to rain on the way over to the squash court—a sweet encompassing deluge. We parked and got out and were soaked before we got inside.

And it was eerie in the court: the rain on the roof, thunder muted by the walls. Now and then the lights flickered. Yolanda hit the ball as well as I did. We were about even. We traded crosscourts into the deep corners, hit odd angles, drop shots, rails. We rallied for a half hour, and in the midst of this, the door opened from the outside.

"Is that you in there, Tom?"

It was Will Fordham.

"It is," I said.

He clambered up the ladder to the gallery, but I didn't look around. Yolanda and I hit several more shots, a reverse corner, a lob, a series of boasts.

Will's footsteps retreated. The door opened. There was a pause, and then the lights went off, and the door slammed closed.

We waited a moment in the pitch darkness. The white walls were black, the lines invisible. I felt the floor beneath us, but that was all. The rain on the roof diminished to a whisper. I heard Yolanda step to the right side wall and move back to the center. I loped forward as if I were retrieving a ball she had hit, and edged back to the tee. She lunged for my return. This went on for several minutes. I felt my own labored breath and heard hers. The air moved between us. Then I sidestepped to the wall and grazed her arm with mine.

We both stopped still. I reached my hand into the darkness, found the edge of her sweaty shirt. She touched my damp arm. I heard her sigh. She slid her hand up my arm and across my shoulder to my cheek, across my cheek to my lips. I opened my mouth, tasted the sweat on her palm.

We left the court before dusk and drove up East Bay toward the Battery. The rain had stopped, and the streets glistened in the evening light. On the right were the pale pink and blue and green houses of Catfish Row, and to our left, the Yacht Club and marina. The sea across to Fort Sumter and beyond was roiled in whitecaps.

I turned down Church Street to my parents' house—the white house with the fenced yard, kept immaculately—and stopped in the middle of the street. "That's where I came from," I said.

"I know where you came from," she said. "Do you know where I came from?"

We turned again and came out on South Battery where the immense old houses overlooked the live oaks in Civil War Park. The air was humid and hot, and a silver mist rolled up from the seawall in the last of the sun.

Suddenly we were caught in a line of cars.

"It's Saturday," Yolanda said.

"What's Saturday?"

"Look," she said.

People surged across the street both ways, streamed through the cars parked at the curb and the ones in the street, around the oleanders near the seawall. Everyone in the park and on the sidewalks and on the battery was black.

"Will you walk with me?" Yolanda asked.

I parked in Duke Maxwell's driveway, and we made our way across the street through the stopped cars. I hadn't been to the park in a while. There were the same old cannons and plaques to soldiers and monuments to dead generals sheltered by live oaks. People seethed around us—teenagers, women in shorts, a man in a turban, groups of young men in fishnet shirts playing boom boxes. A man in a brown suit nodded to us; a woman offered us a drink from a brown bag. Yolanda drank and made a face and passed the bottle to me. I held the bottle up in toast and drank, too.

We climbed the steps to the battery where the breeze cooled us and the mist was in our faces. There was too much noise to talk—music, voices, people everywhere. Lights blinked from across the water through the dusk. I took Yolanda's hand, dazed and joyful and delirious with the sensation of being new.

One day that fall I had just checked my post office box for applications to law schools—I was thinking about what to do next—and I ran into Rachel on Broad Street. She was dressed in a business suit and was on her way to show her work to an art gallery. We bought two cups of coffee at a street vendor's cart and sat on a bench in the park across from St. Michael's.

"I heard about your father," she said, stirring her coffee. "How is he?"

"He's all right. He's in Alaska with my mother."

"Will said you quit the real-estate business."

I nodded. "I'm at loose ends," I said. "I think I will be for a while."

"I'm sorry you haven't called."

"I couldn't," I said.

"Everyone *knows,* Tom. You don't think you have a secret?"

"No," I said. "My mother knows. I don't think I have a secret."

"I'd have thought you of all people would want to get away."

I smiled at this and looked at the people passing on the sidewalk close by. It was a warm day, and the sidewalk was crowded. "This is where I'm from," I said. "You have to be from somewhere." I sipped my coffee. "What about you? How do you like Charleston?"

She shrugged. "It's like a small town. People judge you."

"There are consequences to everything," I said.

We talked a little more—about her painting, the hurricane season coming, Sarah's redecorating the house. She looked at her watch, then stood up and tossed her empty cup into the trash bin. "I have to be there in five minutes."

I stood up, too.

"Whatever happened to that friend of yours?" she asked. "The one who showed up at the dance."

"Alton Maddox?"

She nodded.

"He's somewhere photographing cranes."

She nodded, then looked at me closely. "What if you'd spoken up that night, Tom? What if you'd said, 'Here I am' when he'd called to you?"

"I don't know," I said.

Rachel smiled and touched my arm. It was a kind gesture, not one of blame. She meant she understood you could only do at the moment what you had the courage to. Then she gave me a quick embrace, and we wished each other luck.

She walked one way, up Broad, and I walked the other. The sun was not quite to noon, and the buildings on the south side of the street were in shadow. At the intersection, the high white spire of St. Michael's ran its shadow down onto the sidewalk. I crossed over into the sun. Rachel's asking about Alton made me think back to the photographs he'd taken of Yolanda that day at the squash court, or not to the photographs so much as that he knew she was there—she was the reason he got his camera out. He used Will and me as the excuse. He knew what to look at. That was his gift. He envisioned the larger world and believed in himself enough to love the right things. I smiled, then, thinking what I said afterward to Clarice—that I was not Alton's keeper. But I *was* Alton's keeper, and Yolanda's; and they were mine.